Rules
of the
Heart

CLOVER AUTREY

Copyright © 2024 Clover Autrey

This book is a work of fiction. Names, characters, places, and incidents either are products of the author's imagination or are used fictitiously.
Published by Red Rover Books
Kineograph animation art created by Jess Weiss
Cover art photos legally licensed through Dreamstime.com
All rights reserved.

ISBN-9798327024731

TO THE RULE KEEPERS
WITHOUT YOU THERE WOULD BE CHAOS

TO THE RULE BREAKERS
WHO ARE BRAVE ENOUGH TO NOT ALWAYS GO WITH WHAT'S EXPECTED

TO BEING BOTH AT ONE TIME
OR ANOTHER
SOMEHOW KNOWING WHEN TO
BE A KEEPER OR A BREAKER

HIGHLAND SORCERY
HIGHLAND SORCERER
HIGHLAND EMPATH
HIGHLAND SHAPESHIFTER
HIGHLAND MOON SIFTER
HIGHLAND SORCERY CHRISTMAS
HIGHLAND SON
HIGHLAND ILLUSION
HIGHLAND SOLDIER
HIGHLAND CHIEFTAN

CHAPEL PINES
RULES OF THE HEART
FRAGILE IS THE HEART
A HEART FOR KEEPS
A HOME FOR HIS HEART
FOLLOW HIS HEART
STUBBORN IS THE HEART

ARMY RANGER BILLIONAIRES
RAPTOR
TEA
SANDMAN
RASCAL
TRICKSTER
CHICK

RULES OF THE HEART

"*HE UP* and left her at the altar."

With the phone cradled between his shoulder and cheek, B. "Dance" McCagan's fingers paused on the computer keyboard. What was he supposed to say to that? And where was Shannon? His sister should be working the reservation desk, not him. She would handle this so much better. "You want to cancel the Honeymoon Suite then?" was all he could think to ask.

"Yes, of course I want to...hold the line a

minute." The woman on the other end of the phone started talking to someone else barely out of his earshot. A few watery replies in the negative was all he made out. "No, you need it," the caller overrode whoever she was speaking with and then she was back on the line with him. "We'll keep the reservation and add another room, a double please. We're all coming."

"All?" He actually felt creases furrowing in his brow. What did *all* mean when a wedding was called off? Surely the groom wouldn't still be—?

"All us bridesmaids and the bride." Her tone indicated that should be obvious because what else does a jilted bride do but go on her honeymoon with the wedding party? "We'll be there this evening."

Perplexed, Dance scheduled the extra room, only remembering after the call ended that he hadn't gotten the new credit card information. Everything was still in the groom's name, one Marcus Wentworth. He left a note in the computer for Chalese to get that straightened out when the party arrived tonight. Fortunately, he'd be watching the game with the guys over at Sooty's Grill by the time the bedraggled bride and her bevy of bridesmaids arrived.

"What's with the look?" Shannon stood at the end of the reservation counter, holding a large arrangement of fresh red roses. He hadn't heard her walk in from the back through the dining area.

Coming out from behind the long wooden counter, Dance ignored her question and took the flowers from her. "What are all these?"

"They're for the honeymooners coming in. I thought they'd add a romantic touch to the room."

Dance winced. "About that."

Shannon frowned. "They didn't cancel, did they?" She'd put a lot of effort into advertising the romantic suite to bring in more honeymooner business.

"Well. One of them did."

"One of them?" Her nose wrinkled like it had since she'd been two. "They're not coming together?" Her shoulders sagged. "They called off their wedding last minute. That's horrible. Which one's still coming?"

"Bride. And bringing the support of all of her bridesmaids."

"Oh gosh." Shannon hurried around the counter to get at the computer. "You didn't keep them in the Honeymoon Suite, did you? You did! Dance!"

He set the flowers down on the tall mahogany counter. "That's what they booked."

Shannon was shaking her head, fingers tapping the keyboard. "She cannot stay in there. Think about it. It will just remind her of *him*." The last word came out harshly. "And what tonight was supposed to be. No, we're putting them in the Sam Houston Presidential Suite and the adjoining Yellow Rose room, the one with the balcony that looks out over the lake. And we're only charging them a regular room's rate."

"But..."

Her scowl cut him off. "Some things are more important than money."

He sighed. That's not what he was going to say. Even while they were bouncing back from last year's downturn on top of their mom's mounting medical costs. They'd agreed to tighten the proverbial belt rather than have to let any of their staff go until they got the inn back to where she'd been in previous years. The jewel of the hill country.

"We'll need to switch out the gift basket too, change the dinner menu from romantic to something upbeat..." Shannon's brow puckered in determination.

Dance curled his hand over hers, stopping hers on the keyboard. "I can take care of this. You don't have to."

Her head snapped up, green eyes bright. "This isn't about me."

"I know."

She huffed. "It's not." Her fingers were

cold beneath his, chilled from the sudden rush of blood dropping to her toes.

"I said, I know." Better than anyone. It'd been his shoulder she'd cried on when Richard walked out of their marriage six months ago. His fists still clenched every time he thought of the jerk, aching to smash his face in. Again. Once was clearly not enough. But Richard deserved it. Stepping out on Shannon. And worse, the deadbeat didn't stick around to be a father to Brighton. What kind of man walked out on his three-year-old daughter? "Let me take care of this for you."

"Look." Shannon shifted to face him. "I know what you're thinking, but believe me, I can handle this. I'm a big girl now. Every little reminder of a jerk isn't going to send me howling like a loon off the pier. Besides, any way I can make this weekend better for this bride, it will be like sticking it to Richard. So, get out of here and let me do my thing."

Dance didn't budge.

Shannon rolled her eyes so hard he was surprised the ligaments didn't squeak. "Go." Her attention turned back to the computer, fingers tapping. "Oh, just a thought." Recognizing the sudden tilt of her head for what it was, he realized he shouldn't have lingered. "Maybe you and Wyatt could hang around this weekend even while you're off shift. Maybe have the guys over."

"What for? I'm meeting them tonight—oh I get it. No way."

"Oh, come on." Shannon stopped typing to access him over the top of the monitor. "Having attractive men around will take the sting out of being dumped. Show her there's better fish in the pond. You don't have to do anything, just hang around and look pretty."

He coughed out a laugh at that. Only Shannon. Shaking his head, he threw their younger brother under the bus. "I'm sure Wyatt will be more than happy to take you up on that. In fact, I'll go ask him."

"You do that. And while you're at it, order one of the cheese and rolls baskets Heather makes for their room to go with the complimentary wine."

That he could do for her. "They're going to love it. Forget honeymooners, the inn will become the new hot spot for jilted brides and grooms."

"I hope not." Shannon frowned. "I just want to make it nice for her, give her a chance to leave here in better spirits than when she arrives."

"If anyone can pull that off, it's you." Leaning in, Dance kissed the top of Shannon's head. "I'll help any way I can."

Shannon's countenance lit.

He whipped a palm up. "Short of standing around and looking pretty."

"Aw but you'd be so good at it." She mock pouted.

He threw his hands up in surrender and backed out of the lobby. "Not happening."

"Chicken," she muttered with a grin.

As he walked, Dance dug out his cell phone and quickly called Heather and ordered not one, but two of her largest cheese and rolls baskets to be delivered tonight. He couldn't help himself, not after seeing Shannon's determination to make things better for the bride. No matter what she said, he knew she was still reeling over Richard and how quickly and easily he'd taken off after she'd thrown him out. Even after everything the guy had done, Dance knew his sister well enough to know she'd hoped for a happy ending, that when she kicked him out, he'd come to his senses, and come back to her a changed man. Shannon was too much of a romantic not to believe in second chances. Too good of a mom to not want the father of her child in Brighton's life. The jerk had thrown away the best two things in his life. And though Shannon hid her broken heart behind wry humor and quick grins, Dance saw through to all the tiny broken pieces barely holding his sister together. So yeah, he'd gone ahead and ordered two of the baskets. The second would come out of his own wallet. What of it?

He found Wyatt in the wide sunroom behind the kitchen with their mother and Brighton working on a jigsaw puzzle. Wyatt sat on the edge of a rocker, dark hair hanging low over his eyes as he stared at the brightly colored pieces scattered across the wicker coffee table. Since their mom's stroke, they'd discovered that working on puzzles seemed to help. Sometimes. This one looked rather difficult, a bouquet of blossoms without much pattern to differentiate the pieces.

What a picture they made. Brighton's riot of light brown curls overpowered her head. He'd never seen a child with so much hair and next to Wyatt's darker hair it looked even brighter.

"That's the wrong one. Blues go with blues."

Brighton jammed two blue pieces together that clearly didn't interlock right and set them in the middle of the table and shot Wyatt a look daring him to tell her she was wrong.

His mom was frowning, her posture tense, fingers crabbing as she tried to work a piece into place. A little pang sheared off a piece of Dance's worried heart. Elise McCagan used to be able to work puzzles in her sleep. Frustration wore heavy in her features, erasing the vibrancy she carried just six months ago.

"Let me help you, Mom." Wyatt took the piece from her hand, studied it and handed it back to her. "You just need to turn it to fit."

Rather than place the piece, she dropped it and leaned back in her chair, disinterested.

So, it was one of those days. Her therapist, Shawnie, had warned them about the change in moods and temper, but sometimes their mom seemed like an entirely different person.

Dance walked around the large planter

of peonies and gave her a peck on the cheek. "Hi, Mom."

She blinked up at him, frowning, then looked away out the large, screened windows.

Wyatt looked up at him, his face neutral, conveying in that silent way of brothers what Dance already surmised. Mom wasn't having a good day. Dance crouched down by her chair. "Do you want to go for a walk outside today?"

"I do." Brighton piped up, puzzle already forgotten.

Their mom didn't so much as acknowledge the question.

"There's a cool breeze coming off the lake."

She shook her head. "I'm tired."

At least they'd get her to walk back to her room. That was something. She'd already made such great progress, walking every day, getting her out of the wheelchair, but embarrassment of her dragging leg or the way her words mixed when speaking, kept her from venturing outdoors or in the heavily utilized areas of the inn. The past couple of weeks, she seemed to be going backwards in the progress she'd made.

"Let's get you to your room then."

"No walk?" Brighton's bottom lip poked out irresistibly. She had all three of her uncles wrapped around her chubby little finger and knew it.

Wyatt swooped her up. "We'll go for a walk, honey. You and me around the lake."

She squealed happily, hugging Wyatt around the neck. Having him home was a Godsend. The moment Dance had called about their mom, Wyatt had arranged for his partner to handle his clients at the firm in Dallas and drove down to help out. He'd been making the commute ever since, working in Dallas three days a week and spending the rest of the time here.

Between Wyatt, him and Shannon, and Chloe making it out every other weekend from college, there was someone always available to be with their mother. And once Cash got back from the archeological dig in Peru, the entire family would be on hand. Poor kid had been frantic, ready to give up the spot he'd worked so hard to get to come home. Only Shannon's reassurance that she was being taken care of and she wouldn't want him to give up his internship kept Cash from racing home. He emailed every week, calling when he could get to a phone.

"Come on, Mom." Dance helped her to her feet where she leaned on his arm for a moment to get her footing pointed in the right direction.

The walk to her room was slow. She'd moved into the inn a few years ago, claiming the house was too big and lonely without Dad, but they all knew she wanted to give the house to Shannon and Richard to help them make ends meet until Richard got back on his feet after being let go at the cannery. Now it was Shannon and Brighton's home.

As he and his mom made their way down the

hall, Dance tried to engage her in conversation, but she had clammed up on him. Instead, he filled in the silence with details about the inn, finding himself telling her about the jilted bride and her party who were coming in and how he worried about it affecting Shannon. He hoped to draw his mom out, but she was closing up on all of them. His throat tightened at the thought. What would they all do without the force of nature that was Elise McCagan?

He settled her into bed. It was her bed from home they'd brought over along with all her knick-knacks from places she and Dad had visited. They always came home claiming The McCagan was the finest inn across the country. Dance smiled faintly at the recollection. "Do you want me to rub your arms for you?"

She shook her head. "Just..." She stopped, frustration welling in her eyes as she struggled for the word that should be so simple yet was out of her grasp. She'd said it less than fifteen minutes ago. How could it be gone so quickly?

Tired. Dance wanted to say it for her, help her in any way that he could.

Lips pressed together, she turned her head away, closing in on herself.

He pulled the blanket up around her shoulders. "I'll check in on you before I head out for the night. Shawnie will be here in a few hours for your therapy."

She didn't respond in any way, nor did Dance expect her to.

Several hours later, Dance was running behind. After an influx of unscheduled arrivals for the weekend, he headed to his mom's room to check on her. Shawnie had it all under control with the television tuned to his mom's favorite evening drama as a distraction while she worked and massaged tight muscles to keep them from spasming.

Shawnie was a perfect fit for mom's changing temperament. Working on her internship, she took a few evening jobs after her shift at the medical center.

He made it to the lobby just as the wedding party he'd hoped to avoid blew in through the large oaken doors. Four women in all, still dressed to the nines in pastel tulle, laughing and boisterous, who'd obviously been toasting to the groom's early demise before they arrived.

All but one.

Obviously, the bride as she wasn't in a matching bridesmaid dress but had changed into jeans and a soft blue T-shirt. The casual wear was in complete contrast to the artfully crafted up-do piled on her head.

Unlike the rest of her party, she was stone cold sober. If a bit dazed. She looked around the lobby, dark lashes blinking sluggishly. Her eyes caught on Dance momentarily and his breath faltered at the shine of sadness he glimpsed before her attention moved on.

Dance's gaze remained fixed on her, anger coming at him from left field. It felt as though someone whacked a baseball bat smack in the center of his chest.

What kind of man left a woman like that at the altar?

"You must be Constance." Shannon scurried out from the dining room, making a beeline straight to the would-be bride, gripping her by the arms. "You poor thing. What a day you've had."

Dance rubbed his brow, wondering why his sister was still here instead of home with Brighton. She could deny it all she wanted, but this jilting business had gotten to her.

Shannon slung her arm around *Constance's* shoulder—best buddies in five seconds flat. Had to be a record. "Would you like to go to your rooms first or straight to dinner? We have a lovely table set up for you."

"Dinner."

"Rooms please." A couple of the bridesmaids called out simultaneously and then leaned on each other, laughing about it.

"I think I'd like a few minutes first," Constance said. Tired little wisp looked ready to drop where she stood. and Dance felt a sudden need to take care of her.

He tamped that down before it could take root. He didn't even know her. Time to stop standing there and make his own beeline toward the exit.

"Oh, Dance. I thought you left already," Shannon called out and five sets of feminine eyes latched onto him. He hadn't been fast enough.

"I was just…" He pointed lamely toward the door.

"Would you be a darling and show the ladies up to the suite while I go over a few details with Constance?" Shannon used her sugary tone on him.

"Uh…sure," he said. He knew what

Shannon was doing. She wouldn't bother a distraught woman with details she already had handled. She was offering the woman a few private moments away from her overly helpful girlfriends who most likely had been sympathizing her to insanity for several hours. It wouldn't kill him to help her out in that small measure.

"Yeah, Dreamboat, be a darling and take us up to the suite."

Or maybe it would kill him.

One of the bridesmaids with a purple stripe dyed in her platinum hair, latched onto his arm. He recognized her voice as the straightforward one who had called earlier this morning. Another glommed onto his other arm and Dance found himself surrounded front and back, side-to-side, by the giggling tipsy brood.

"This way, ladies." He herded them toward the elevator, his legs hemmed in by a frothy sea of tulle.

TWO

HIS MOOD had soured considerably by the time he made it to Sooty's Grill. The game was in full swing, blasting from the flatscreen that took up most of the end wall at the side of the scuffed bar counter.

"Dance." Wyatt waved him over to their standard table where most of their Friday night pals were already gathered and gaping with rapt interest at the game. Dance barely glanced at the score as he made his way through the crowd and yeasty smell of fresh beer. Peanut shells crunched beneath his boots.

Wyatt nudged a full glass his way when he sat. "Hear tell you didn't make it past the gaggle of bridesmaids." His brother's grin was unrepentant.

"No, I did not." Dance shuddered. They'd had him in the suite a full ten minutes before he managed to wrangle himself away. "How'd you escape from Shannon?"

"Offered to take Brighton home until Chloe got there to take over. You should have thought of it. Getting slow on the uptake, bro."

"Chloe's in town?" From his other side, Levi asked before taking a quick pull of his beer, eyes fixed on the television.

"Came in for the weekend again," Wyatt answered, grabbing a handful of peanuts. Levi and Wyatt had been friends forever, both enlisting at the same time, though Wyatt had come back from Afghanistan more or less intact, Levi returned with part of his arm missing below the elbow and scars up and down his left side. Wyatt had been with him through rehab every painful step of the way. As close as they were, Wyatt seemed blinded by Levi's interest in Dance and Wyatt's baby sister. Either that or he just didn't want to think about it. And since Chloe was just as dense to Levi's attraction, Wyatt didn't have to worry about it.

Not that Dance wanted to broach the obvious either. Levi would either decide to stake a claim or he wouldn't. It was no-nevermind to him.

"Hey, did that shipment for the carriage house come in yet?" He asked Levi about an easier topic. They hired him to refurbish the old carriage house into guest rooms, not only because he'd outbid everyone else, but because he was a true craftsman with an eye for detail. He could be trusted to keep the carriage house true to her one-hundred-year-old history. It was going to be beautiful.

"The shipment? Should be in by Monday so I can get back to work on it."

"So, were any of them worth looking at?" Wyatt raised his brows. John and Austin pulled their attention from the game.

"What? The shipment of cedar?"

"The wedding gals," Austin supplied. His red hair was slicked down on the crown from wearing his hat all day while riding in his crop harvester.

"Oh, um…yeah. They are all very pretty." Actually, Dance hadn't really noticed, had barely paid attention to any of them after seeing Constance. Her image filled the forefront of his mind, how she'd stood there so forlorn, blond ringlets pinned above a sad angel's face. The truth was he hadn't even looked at the other girls. But…if the guys were interested in hanging around the inn, it would free him from Shannon pushing him towards the bridesmaids as a distraction. "Leastways, they were all dolled up for a wedding."

"That's the best way to meet women." Austin leaned back. "At weddings when they're feeling all romantic and lonely. Except for the jilted bride. Too soon for her unless you're into tears and hearing about how she's been done wrong. Stay clear of that one. But the rest are fair game."

"And ready to find husbands," Wyatt chimed in. "Trust me. When one gets married, they all start thinking about it. No thank you, ma'am."

"Maybe that's what some of us want." Austin grinned.

They all threw peanuts at him, groaning and shuddering at the unwanted sentiment.

"What?" Austin brushed a peanut off his shoulder. "This is great, guys, really, but I don't intend to look at your ugly mugs every Friday the rest of my life."

John snagged an elbow around Austin's neck and pulled his head down for a hard knuckle rub. "You wouldn't last two weeks before you'd be crawling back."

"Touchdown!" The bar erupted and all talk of women and marriage was forgotten as their team continued to dominate the field.

But the excitement of the game was lost for Dance. He couldn't get into it as his mind played out the scenario of Constance walking down the aisle in a cloud of satin, her heart-shaped face glowing with happiness, then melting into shock as a faceless jerk wasn't present, had left her facing the preacher alone.

How could any man do that to a woman? Embarrass her like that? How could a guy have let it get to that point? He didn't know anything about this Marcus Wentworth, except that he was too much of a coward to man up and call it off before the day of the wedding.

Constance hadn't gotten a good look at the inn last night. She'd been too numb, shell-shocked from yesterday's turn of events that was supposed to be the happiest day of her life.

Dru, Beth and Annette dragged her to the inn—quite heavy-handedly—because everything beyond Marcus's note that he'd left for her in the church's bridal room was a blur. He'd scrawled in an obviously hurried hand...*I can't do this. Sorry.*

The inn had provided a wonderful dinner of braised walnut stuffed chicken and yams last night and her friends had imbibed in a little too much of the local wine. Constance's first sip had flattened in her churning stomach.

In their attempt to lighten the heartache for her, her friends hadn't realized she wasn't drinking. She was already too numb for any buzz to do any good.

Now in the early light of day, she was clear-headed and restless. While her bridesmaids were all soundly drooling into their pillows, she slipped out for some much-needed fresh air.

She gave a polite nod to the bright blond woman behind the front desk as she wandered through the stylish entryway and pushed through one of the two wide front doors to go outside.

This early in the morning the Texas air was cool and peaceful. Several different kinds of birds were chirping back and forth in the feathery tufted leaves of the mimosa trees draping over each end of the inn's polished white portico porch. The silky pink pom-pom blossoms spritzed the air with the fragrance that made her think of fruit punch.

Stepping down the wide steps, Constance inhaled the air and looked back at the two-story Antebellum inn. It really was like stepping back into another era.

Off the side of the circular driveway, she found a meandering pathway of cobblestones. She took that around the side of the inn through a flower garden of awakening peonies and bright yellow daffodils that instantly lightened her mood. She followed the path around a sunroom that spanned the entire side of the inn to the back where the wrap-around porch stepped down to a lovely expanse of lawn broken in half by a wide dirt pathway that led to a private lake. The strip of sandy tan beach and a gazebo built on posts that extended partway over the water invited a sense of serenity that Constance yearned for.

On the far side, before the rolling hills, weeping willows hugged the edge of the lake with delicate branches swaying in the slight breeze like a line of ballerinas moving their arms in graceful synchronization and Constance felt a thin layer of haze sweep away from her heart.

It felt like she'd taken her first real breath since yesterday. Dru had been right to bring her here. Not so much to party her woes away, but this place; it was peaceful. It spoke to her soul.

With no one else about yet, she imagined the lake was her own private paradise. Away from where all her wedding guests gawked at her in sympathy, and where her mother didn't ask what she'd done to drive such a catch as Marcus away.

Constance closed her eyes and let the warm breeze and the chatter of the birds wash it all away.

Gosh, what a day yesterday had been.

But she'd survived it and today was fresh and new.

Letting her eyes slide open, she took another longing look at the lake and the rolling hills beyond. There was a private winery at the edge of the property. She could make out the neat rows of grapevines in the distance as she made a slow turn to take everything in. On the other side of the inn from the garden area she'd come through, was an old barn or what they called the carriage house according to the brochures she and Marcus had looked at.

The sun rising behind it showered the building in a golden glow. It wasn't open to guests yet, but she just had to go over there, see if she could take a peek inside one of the windows. The pathway widened to a wide flat stone area in front of the rolling style barn doors. They were large enough for a carriage to drive through. The flagstones looked like they'd been recently placed. The soil between them matched the rich dirt in the flower beds along the side of the building, just waiting for seedlings to be planted. Whoever was doing the landscaping had an eye in keeping with the quiet natural beauty and settled feel of the place.

The windows were old and coated in the yellowing dinge of years. They'd probably have to be replaced or treated somehow. They weren't much good for looking through either, though Constance gave it a good try in her attempt to wipe away decades of Texas baked-on clay. All she could see was a dim gritty smear.

Constance stepped back, eyeing the building in her determination to get a look inside. The large doors hung on casters that rolled open and closed…and oh, they weren't flushed together. That small gap might give her that peek inside.

Excellent. Her aunts said she was too nosy for her own good, but right now having something else to occupy her mind over stupid Marcus was a saving grace to her sanity. And everyone thought she'd be the one to call off the wedding.

Her fingers paused on the door.

Why had everyone joked about that? What

had they noticed about her and Marcus that she'd been oblivious to?

Constance pressed her nose at the gap between the huge doors, bracing her hands on them when one of them shifted. Oh gosh. It wasn't locked.

She drew back, hesitant. She really shouldn't go in. It was trespassing. And this was Texas. They actually shoot people out here for that, didn't they?

She scraped her bottom lip between her teeth. Aw, screw it. She'd been left at the altar, humiliated in front of everyone she knew, her mom acted like it was somehow her fault. Getting caught in the carriage house couldn't be any worse.

She slid the door open only enough to squeeze through, pleasantly surprised that the casters didn't squeal and give her away.

The interior was massive, much larger than it had appeared from the outside. It looked large enough to house several carriages in its day, with enough stalls to hold half again as many horses.

The dewy sunlight filtered in through high

pane-less windows near the rafters, slashing the muted dark with slanting streamers of light.

It created one heck of an atmosphere. Constance sighed, breathing in the peace that was here and slid the door open a little more to allow in more of the light.

Signs of ongoing construction were everywhere. Sawhorses, hammers, toolboxes, a cutting saw… It looked like one wall of the stalls had been taken apart, not with a sledgehammer, for the old partitions were still intact and stacked against the wall. She wondered if they were going to be re-used in the carriage house somehow. The attention to historic detail and use of local materials was something that had drawn her to honeymoon at the inn itself. She imagined the stall walls as a perfect door to a washroom, or headboard, or two of them paired for an interesting outdoor courtyard divider. Her interior designer's heart was sparking with the possibilities.

Everything else was laid out in heaps.

An industrial garbage can had been brought in for obvious waste to be hauled out, but there were also piles of scrap wood and metal, and another pile of items that appeared were set aside to be refurbished later like the stall partitions or to be gone through by the owners of the inn. There were old feeding buckets, horseshoes, and other equipment for taking care of horses. Lots of leather hasps and bridles and some things she had no idea of their use. A couple dusty trunks she'd love to open and see what was in them, and…wonder what was in that? She zeroed in on a small flat box about the length of a man's hand. It stuck out a few inches from one of the feeding buckets that was tipped on its side as though someone had tossed the box in it without much thought, which made the bucket fall over.

She'd no sooner picked it up when a voice startled her from behind.

"This building is off-limits to guests." A deep southern drawl echoed in the room.

Constance swung around, holding the box to her chest.

It was the dark-haired guy from last night who showed her bridesmaids to their rooms. He obviously worked at the inn, although he hadn't been in the white shirt and dark slacks all the staff wore, but in jeans and a casual shirt. Same as now except the white shirt had been exchanged for a long-sleeved shirt left unbuttoned over a faded blue T-shirt. Everything else had been so dulled to her all she really remembered about him was that he was the first person all day who hadn't looked at her with sympathy. He'd actually seemed a little angry. Not at her, she didn't think. Why would he be? But it had been refreshing nonetheless to look up and see a different emotion than the pity that had been directed at her for hours.

He didn't seem angry now, even though he'd caught her going through things that didn't belong to her.

"Oh sorry." She clutched the flat box

tighter, unwilling to give it up until she saw what was inside. "I just…okay, the truth is, I couldn't resist coming in here. It's so beautiful."

A dark eyebrow lifted. He glanced around the space.

"Construction chaos aside, it is. Just the structure alone, and the light. And all right, my family says I'm too curious for my own good, well the word they use is nosy, but I had a bad day yesterday, really bad—"

"I know."

That brought her rambling up short. Great, even here everybody knew of her humiliation. Why would she think otherwise? The entire inn's staff probably figured that out when she showed up minus one groom and three bridesmaids instead.

"Oh, um, well." Now she felt really awkward. "I couldn't stay in the suite any longer. I had to get out and it looked so peaceful in here. I just really needed a few moments…"

"It's okay."

Her gaze snapped up to him. "It is?"

One side of his lip quirked up in the faintest of smiles. "It's fine."

"You're sure? I don't want to get you in trouble with your bosses."

"My...?" Something close to amusement caught in his dark eyes. "My bosses won't mind in the least."

"You're certain?"

"Fairly certain, although I better remain with you just in case."

"In case of what?"

"Accident. Liability. This *is* a construction zone."

Oh. Right. She really would rather be alone, but she could see his point. "In case one of those rafters that have managed to stay intact more than a few centuries decides at this precise moment in time to fall on my head?"

She got a full-on grin out of him with that and had to admit it looked nice on him. He had the sort of face that looked like it wasn't home to many smiles so she felt a little proud that she'd garnered one so quickly. It was her best attribute: getting others to lighten up. It was one of the things Marcus loved about her. He said she always managed to make him feel better in any situation. Wonder how he was feeling now?

"What is that?" The guy nodded toward the box she held.

"I don't know. It was in this pile. Stuff to be gone through later, it seems."

"That you thought you'd go through first?" His eyes were teasing.

She smiled. She'd love to sort through all this stuff. She shrugged. "I was just..."

"Curious?" he said.

"It's all right. You can say nosy. I own up to it."

"Would it help you to know that I thought it?" He grinned.

Oh, she liked his wry barely there humor. She chuckled. "It does." Having someone treat her like a normal person instead of an emotional basket case helped.

"Well then. Let's be nosy together." He walked over to her, his boots sounding on the floorboards, and held out his hand.

Reluctantly, she gave over the box.

But he surprised her by just holding it, clasp out, and nodded. "Go ahead."

"Really?" She grinned up at him. Now that he was close, she noticed how tall he was, a good head taller than her. Even taller than Marcus. And really nice. The gesture of letting her open the box brightened what was sure to be another difficult day.

"Are you going to open it?"

"I am. I just want to savor it for a while longer because once it's opened, the expectation of something amazing inside is gone."

He chuckled. "Considering it's been in an old carriage house for who knows how long—I've never even seen this before and I've... *worked...*

here a long time—I wouldn't hold your expectations high. It's probably empty. Just an old box."

"I know all that. Which is why I'm taking my time."

"Then by all means, take as long as you need."

She eyed him but found no mockery. He really was letting her savor the moment. Patient guy. Of course she was a guest at the inn. All the employees so far were the type who went overboard to accommodate their guests. Even heartbroken messes like herself. A little pang tapped her heart. Pathetic. She had to stop thinking about Marcus. He didn't love her. Probably never really had.

She looked down at the box, trying to bring back the enthusiasm of discovery.

The guy's thumbs absently tapped the top of the box. Okay not as patient as he was letting on, which made her smile and loosened the tightness in her chest a bit. She had to admit it was much more fun having a partner-in-crime. Besides, they were just snooping. They weren't going to take anything.

She flicked the little antique latch open with her fingernail and lifted the lid.

"Oh my gosh!"

All thoughts of Marcus vanished at the discovery. She couldn't believe it.

"What?"

He leaned down for a closer look, and she jerked up. *Smack.* The back of her head whacked into his.

"Gah." He stumbled back, and then bent over, holding his nose.

Constance managed to hang onto the box. "Are you okay?" She bent to look into his face and winced. His nose was bleeding.

His sideways glance at her was incredulous.

"You wroke my nose."

She stifled a grin at how ridiculous he sounded. She closed the box so the contents wouldn't spill out. "I highly doubt that. We couldn't have hit that hard. My head barely hurts."

Again, he gave her that dubious sidewise look. "How wondervul for you."

A bubble of laughter hiccupped out. "I'm sorry."

"I can tell."

"No, really." She covered her mouth to hold any more pips of laughter in and glanced around for something to staunch the blood.

"Wour concern warms me." He straightened, scowling.

She bit her lip to hold back the laughter that wanted to come out. It really wasn't funny, not in the least, but she couldn't help it. *It was funny.* And it felt so gosh darn good to laugh, a needed release. She found some unopened painter towels, set the box on the sawhorse, and burrowed a hole in the plastic to pull a few of the towels out.

"Here, use this." She handed him one of the towels to press to his nose. "Tip your head back. We should get you somewhere to clean this off, see how bad this is. If it really is broken…"

"Come with me and wring that." He pointed toward the sawhorse.

"I don't think we should take it out of here. Except maybe we better take it to the front desk. I wouldn't want to just leave it out here now that we know what's in it."

His brows drew down over his hand holding the cloth to his nose.

"You didn't see?" she asked.

"I was a wittle woccupied by the back of your head colliding into my face."

"I said I'm sorry."

He frowned, and then slowly nodded, letting it go. "So, what's in there?"

THREE

EXCITEMENT flushed through Constance's chest, the same as it had at her first glimpse inside the box. She could hardly believe what she'd seen. She ran over to the sawhorse and picked up the box, turning, and nearly collided with the guy who had followed her over.

"Oh." She automatically tried to step back but was trapped by the sawhorse.

Realizing he was crowding her, he took a step back, still holding that painter's towel to his face. It was pretty thick and there weren't any spots of red so the nosebleed must be slowing, but he wasn't taking any chances yet.

Watching him to see his reaction,

Constance opened the lid. And wasn't disappointed at the way his eyes widened and jaw dropped open. His eyes lifted from the open box to her in bafflement.

Nestled in faded velvet lay a beautiful antique comb, the curved kind that women used both as adornment and to hold up their hair. This one was exquisite, made of genuine tortoiseshell embedded with tiny blue diamonds, most probably real, flowing along the scalloped edge.

"I know, right?" she said. "Can you believe this was tossed in a pile of junk? That it's been sitting around in this old barn all this time? Where do you think it came from?"

He shook his head. "I have no idea. What's that paper in the lid?"

"Huh?" Constance hadn't seen that, what with banging heads together and all. She twisted the box around. Sure enough, there was a folded sheet of aged paper tucked up inside the lid. "Do you think I should take it out? No." She resisted the urge. "We shouldn't without gloves or something to protect it." As much as she wanted to know what it was, she didn't want to ruin something that didn't belong to her.

"There are plastic gloves in the first-aid kit. Come on." The guy turned on his heel.

That settled it then. They could indulge their curiosity without risk and then hand the comb over to the owners of the inn.

They went into the inn from the back through the large kitchen area where several of the morning kitchen staff smiled and nodded at their fellow employee who was holding the white rag to his face. Puzzled glances followed them out. Constance really hoped he wasn't going to get in trouble for trooping her through the kitchen, but he seemed confident in what he was doing.

He must be part of the senior staff then.

He pushed through into the dining area like he owned the place. She was practically jogging to keep up with his long strides. She held the box tightly to her.

The gal at the registration desk looked up and her eyes widened. "What happened?"

"Wong story." His voice was nasally again, and he was pressing the cloth more firmly to his nose. The bleeding must not have stopped after all. The guy hurried across the lobby toward the office that the inn's owner, Shannon, had taken her into last night for a reprieve from her inebriated bridesmaids.

Constance smiled apologetically when the girl's eyes landed on her. "Bloody nose. He, um, it. Our heads somehow collided." She fled into the office before having to answer to the girl's arched eyebrow.

The guy already had the first aid kit opened on the desk and was rummaging through it with his free hand.

Constance set the antique box down beside the kit. "What are you looking for?"

"Aspirin."

"Let me find it. You sit down and tilt your head forward."

He looked at her dubiously but gave up his search and lowered to the rolling chair.

"You said to hold it back before?"

She shrugged. "I can never remember which is best." She grabbed a couple of little packets in the kit and went through them. "How about this?" She held one of the packets up. "It's powder aspirin so should work faster."

He held out his free hand, but she didn't give it to him yet in favor of looking around. "Do you have anything to drink in here?"

"Bottled water in the fridge." He canted his head to the side and then winced at the movement.

Constance frowned on his behalf and retrieved a bottle of water from the mini fridge that was beside the bookshelf along the wall. She uncapped and set it in front of him and then tore open the little aspirin packet before handing it to him.

"Thank you," he said, before lifting the towel barely enough to pour the powder into his mouth, grimace at the taste and take a quick swallow of water. And another.

Constance sank down in the chair on the opposite side of the desk. "I really am sorry."

He stopped mid-chug to look at her over the cloth he still pressed tight. "It was an accident."

"Yeah but…"

His chuckle was muffled.

"All right," she conceded, and curled her hands around the under sides of her seat to contain her nervous energy. She wanted to see what that note in the box was about yet didn't want to come across overly eager in the face of his injury.

"Has the bleeding stopped?" she blurted. That didn't sound anxious at all.

"No."

"Oh." She looked around the room, anywhere except at the little box with the amazing antique comb inside. She liked this office. It wasn't too big or too small or crowded. The desk was uncluttered, just a few papers and a computer monitor to the side. Except now the opened first aid kit took up the rest of the space.

Nor was it too pristine. The old mahogany desk was scuffed and scratched with an air of usability and character that didn't match the lighter wood of the tall bookshelf. There were a few outdated pictures of the family in small frames and a little plant that didn't take too much space on the shelf. It was a working office, rather than a show place. It was comfortable. The only thing it needed was a window, but since the room was smack-dab in the center of the inn, she guessed that couldn't be helped.

She eyed the guy again. "Maybe you should apply more pressure."

His eyebrows rose. "What do you wink I've been woing?"

She pressed her lips together to keep from laughing but failed.

His response was a bland look.

"I'm sorry, but you sound ridiculous."

"Because I applied more pressure wike you said."

Exasperated, he pulled the towel back an inch. "I think it's stopped. Hang on." Reaching behind him, he grabbed up some paper napkins off the credenza and traded them out for the ruined towel.

"Hand me some of those," Constance ordered, and again he reached behind him and grabbed a handful of the napkins to hand to her. Using his water, she dampened the napkins and gave them back to him to clean up.

"It doesn't look that bad." She eyed him when he was finished, and the cloth and napkins were dumped in the trash can. His nose looked fine. It was his eyes that looked a little off and pinched in pain. Once more she felt the need to apologize. "I'm sorr—"

He cut her off with the lift of his hand. "Accident." He squinted at her. "You're okay, right? No headache?"

She smiled briefly. "Guess I have a hard head. Rotten luck for you."

He grinned back. "I reckon it was some kind of luck at that. Haven't yet decided on exactly what kind." He winked. There was nothing that sent Constance's heart to fluttering like southern charm in the movies. One of the reasons she'd insisted on honeymooning in Texas, and here it was oozing out of a Texan in real life.

She felt the heat of a blush creep up her neck. Whew, maybe she should ask him to turn on the fan. But that would call attention to her pink cheeks. She just knew the blush was visible. Ignoring it in hopes he hadn't noticed, she asked, "Do you think it's okay if we open the letter?"

"I don't see why not?" He took the latex

gloves out of the first aid kit and held them out to her.

"Me?" Without waiting for an answer, she snatched the gloves out of his hand and stretched them on. A sense of giddiness bubbled up inside her. This was as good as finding that perfect item she didn't know she was looking for at the antique market or garage sale.

She opened the box and was again amazed at the stunning comb nestled inside.

She looked across the desk into the guy's eyes. They gleamed with mischief. She suddenly felt a connection with him, like they were in on a treasure hunt together that nobody else knew about. Which was rather fanciful, but right now she needed a little break from the real world. She almost didn't want to open the letter yet, but to prolong the wonder. Sometimes the notion of what could be was better than what was.

She pulled the folded paper from where it was tucked into the top of the box, held all this time by the edges of the lid.

The paper felt thick beneath the gloves. It was folded in thirds. The back third that had rested against the wood of the lid had darkened. Constance hoped it didn't make whatever was written inside unreadable.

If there was anything written at all. She was dying to know who the comb once belonged to and how it had come to be in the carriage house.

"Savoring the moment again?" the guy drawled.

Constance shrugged. "Nervous. What if there's nothing on here?"

The guy's lips tugged downward. "Then we're no worse off than we are right now."

"Yes, we are," she exclaimed with fervor. "Right now, we have hope of any possibility. Once we unfold this piece of paper, that's gone."

"So don't unfold it."

She sat upright. "Then we'll never know."

Amusement crinkled his eyes. "But

you'll retain the possibilities of what could be on it."

She narrowed her eyes. "Well, that's plain stupid. I'm opening it."

"Just as long as you can handle the disappointment." His voice was bland, but, gosh, his eyes were teasing. So much so that the retort that she'd been handling disappointment since her wedding was called off yesterday died in her throat. She was too excited to see what was on this paper to drag Marcus in her thoughts right now.

That did it. No more hesitation. She gingerly unfolded the letter, reveling in the way it crinkled. They may very well be the first people to read it since it was written.

Her heart skipped a beat at the first glimpse of handwriting. It was a short letter, only a few lines, in that old-fashioned swervy cursive.

"*Ady*," Constance read. *"It's with much regret that I cannot return this to you in person.*

I must leave in haste to seek a haven of consolation."

Constance stopped. She looked up at the guy who had come around the desk to read over her shoulder. His features mirrored the sorrow coming from the letter. It felt like they were glimpsing something very private and personal and if Constance wasn't as nosy as she was, she might have stopped reading.

But her curiosity won out. *"I will forever hold you in the fondest esteem and God willing, should my heart ever mend, I will one day seek to return, but at this time I can no longer bear remaining while he is gone from this place.*

"Please know that I will miss you.

"Affectionately yours,

"Peg."

Constance sniffled.

A tear slipped onto her cheek, but she left it alone, rather than wipe it away with the glove and inadvertently smudge the old paper. "That's the saddest thing I've ever read." She sniffled again and suddenly a tissue was in front of her face.

"Thanks," she took it and dabbed at her eyes. "It sounds like some poor woman got her heart broken by some guy, so she took off without even saying goodbye to her friend. That's so horrible."

She dropped the letter into the box and stripped off the gloves so she could really rub at her watery eyes. "What kind of guy does that?" Now that the first tear had leaked out, she couldn't seem to hold back the rest. She hadn't cried over Marcus yet, so why was she suddenly weeping over an old letter that she didn't even know the full story about? This Peg could have gotten back with her man and had her happily ever after and a boatload of children for all she knew. Her shoulders started shaking. This was ridiculous.

A large hand started patting the back of her shoulder, rather awkwardly. "Um, ma'am. Would you like to be alone?"

"No!" She didn't know what possessed her, but abruptly she had hold of his hand and was crying into his sleeve. She didn't know why. He was just comforting in some odd way. And solid. Like a strong sturdy tree she could pour out her heart to and…she froze. What was she doing? Sniffling and crying over a complete stranger's sleeve. Mortification dried up her tear ducts.

She pulled back in her seat, heat burning her cheeks.

"I'm so sorry. I don't know what—" She realized she was still holding his hand and abruptly let go, the burn of embarrassment flushing beneath her skin. She wouldn't be surprised if he tossed her out of the office.

Instead, he crouched down at the side of her chair.

"Dance."

What? She peeked sidewise at him, because…what? "You want to dance?"

"No. That's my name. I thought I should introduce myself since you almost broke my nose and got your make-up all over my sleeve."

"I didn't get my make-up on it." She

glanced at his sleeve to make sure. She hadn't bothered with much mascara this morning.

"Small favors," he drawled, and folded his arms over the arm of her chair. "For what it's worth, I don't know what kind of a man does something like that either."

He said it so sincerely, Constance didn't think he was talking about the contents of the letter. Her throat grew thick. She didn't know what to say to that so went for an easier subject. "Is your name really Dance?"

"Yes, ma'am."

"Not really?" She shook her head, feeling some of the tightness in her chest ease.

"Not really." His grin was small and fleeting. Had she blinked she would have missed it and that would have been a shame. "But I've been called that for as long as I can remember."

"Nickname then."

"Nickname that stuck."

"What's your real name?"

His lips stretched in neutrality, neither a hint of a smile nor a frown. "Something so abominably horrific, it can never be spoken." He placed his palm over his chest.

"Oh, come on. What is it? Percival or something?"

"Percival?" He chuckled. "No."

"Eugene?"

His eyes rolled.

"Maurice?"

"No. And even if it was, I wouldn't tell you."

"So it is Maurice?"

"No."

"That's not fair. If I guess it, you have to tell me."

"I haven't agreed to that."

"So, agree to it. If I guess your name, you tell me."

"You won't guess it."

"So that's a deal?"

He laughed. "Fine."

She would be finding out what it was. "That bad, huh? You know you shouldn't have told that to someone as nosy as me."

"Duly noted."

She let it be for now only because she'd injured him. "So, Dance. Strange nickname. As in get-up-and-boggie?"

"I always thought of it more as a Two-Step kind of name."

She glanced sidewise at him. "You know how to Two-Step?"

His lips creased in a nice smile. "I've been known to."

She nodded, staring at the narrow box in her hand, trying not to think of the first dance she and Marcus were supposed to have danced with every eye on them, cameras flashing, her mom pressing her hands to her heart. Fairy-tale like.

"I could take you." Dance interrupted her downward spiral. He looked concerned. Her thoughts must have shown on her face. "Tonight. I mean all of you. Grab your girlfriends and meet me in the lobby tonight at eight. It looks like you could use some good ole stomping fun."

FOUR

CONSTANCE'S belly fluttered as the inn's complimentary van pulled into the dusty parking lot. The honkey-tonk was exactly as she pictured it. Dance had left a note for them at the front desk, explaining he had an errand with his niece, but would meet them there and had arranged their transportation.

Just on the outskirts of town, the dance hall had an authentic rustic appeal. It was a barn-like structure settled in the dip between two grassy hills. It had wood siding and a metal corrugated roof. The dirt parking lot was filled with pick- up trucks, ranging from spanking off-the-lot new to rust-holding-them-together old. One of them actually had long horns sprouting off the front grill.

"Would you look at this place?" Dru slid out of the van's side door the driver opened for them and stood with her hands planted on her model-bony hips. "Get a load of that sign. The Dance Hall."

She latched onto the driver's arm. He was a wiry old man sporting a long handlebar mustache. "I thought that's what you were just calling it. I didn't think it was the place's name."

"Been The Dance Hall since I was no more than a little sprout climbing a soap box to peek in the windows." He thumbed the brim of his Stetson.

"We have to take pictures in front of it," Beth gushed, pulling out her cell phone.

The driver turned out to be a fair hand at taking a few shots with several different mobile phone cameras. He obviously dealt with tourists wanting snapshots on a regular basis.

Constance had to admit she was having fun mugging it up with her best friends.

Dru, she'd known since eighth grade when she'd come to her rescue with a bleach pen after Blake "the louse" Wright spilled a coke on her sweater. Their personalities were from different planets, but they'd been friends ever since. Beth and Annette were roommates from college. She wouldn't want anyone else but these women with her. Well, except her fiancé. Ex-fiancé, she mentally corrected. The jerk.

The old-timer handed their phones back. "The bartender has my number when you're ready to return. Have him give me a call and a van will be out to collect you, Miss Constance." He tipped his hat. "Ladies." And opened the door for them. Live music wailed from inside.

Beth and Annette grinned at each other and practically scurried inside like excited barnyard mice.

Constance gaped at the scene before her. It was a wide-open space. A packed space. Square bar to the left, the kind where drinks could be served from all sides. Tables and booths lined the space on the other side of the bar.

There was a stage to the far right where a band was playing it up and right in front of them, the rest of the scuffed floor was home to couples gliding across it, moving in counterclockwise circles.

Constance had never seen so many cowboy hats in one place. Men, women. They moved about the floor in an easy glide that resembled the foxtrot—quick, quick, slow, slow—but with a more relaxed hold. A lot of the guys rested their right hands casually on the girl's neck while some of the girls had their thumbs hooked in their partner's back belt loop. There was definitely a casual country air to the smooth rhythm she couldn't quite put a name to.

"Cowboy nirvana," Dru drawled, and Beth giggled.

"Yee haw." Annette twirled her finger in the air. "I need to get me a hat."

"Already located mine." Within three steps Dru

plucked the Stetson right off a lanky red head who was heading for the bar and placed it on her own platinum head. "Hello there, handsome. Want to buy a stranger a drink?"

He looked her up and down, obviously liking what he saw and grinned. "That'd be a downright pleasure, ma'am." Hand on the small of her back, he guided her through the throng of people.

"Wow," Beth said. "She is so bold."

"Always has been." Constance smiled at her friend's retreating back. They watched the dancers for a while, shifting away from the doorway and moving farther into the crowd.

"Should we get a table?" Annette shouted over the music, which had gotten louder as the band switched into a livelier tune.

Constance shrugged, looking for Dance. She wondered if his errand with his niece was taking longer than he'd anticipated. "I guess so."

The energy of the place was incredible. It was as though the entire town was there.

Everyone seemed to know each other. Couples on the dance floor called out in passing, smiling and laughing, some trying to outdo others with spins and dips. She could watch them for hours.

They made their way toward one of the few unoccupied tables that still offered a view of the dance floor when something snagged Constance's wrist.

Turning, she looked up into Dance's handsome features and her belly did that little fluttery thing again. Maybe it was the black cowboy hat settled on his dark hair. Yeah, had to be the cowboy hat.

She frowned, getting a close-up look at him. His nose looked fine, but there was light bruising beneath his eyes. "Are you okay? I didn't break your nose, did I?" She lifted her hand to touch his face but didn't.

His lip cracked a bare smile. "It's not broken. I'm made of sterner stuff than that." He leaned in to be heard over the music. He smelled nice, like piney aftershave. "I have a table for you and your friends over here."

Nodding, Constance grabbed Annette's elbow to get her attention, who in turn took hold of Beth. Constance expected Dance to let go of her wrist but his hand slid down to hers. He led them through the press to a couple of tables that had been pushed together.

A couple of cowboys stood at their arrival. There was a pitcher of beer and several glasses on the table as well as salsa and chips. Dance let go of Constance's hand to pull her chair out. "Ladies, this is my brother Wyatt." He indicated the guy with dark hair and the same walnut-colored eyes as himself, though with far more smile creases at the corners. "And these are Levi and John." Her gaze was instantly drawn down to Levi's shirt sleeve that was folded up around his arm where it ended below the elbow. He also had scars on his cheek and temple that followed the curve of his neck and down into his collar. Looked like he'd been in a terrible accident. "Guys, this is Constance, and…" Lines formed in Dance's forehead.

Constance came to his aid. "These are my…" She almost said bridesmaids. "My friends, Annette and Beth."

"Howdy," John drawled, and Beth blushed. "Turn around the floor?"

Beth blinked and Annette nudged her. "He's asking you to dance. Go on, your Jeff won't mind a few dances."

"Oh." Beth smiled widely. "Love to."

"You game?" Grinning, Dance's brother lifted his elbow for Annette to grasp onto. Without a word passed between them, Annette latched on and they headed to the dance floor.

Suddenly alone with Dance and Levi, Constance was at a loss for what to do. Should she sit down? She really wanted to dance.

She looked up at Dance expectantly. He did invite them all out here after all, and she wasn't going to sit around while all her friends were having fun.

He looked back at her blandly.

Constance rolled her eyes. Seriously? He was going to make her beg? Fine. She wasn't too proud. "Hey…"

"Would you like to dance?" He beat her to it after all.

"Yes." She grinned. "Dying to."

"Great." He took her little clutch and placed it on the table.

"Won't that—?" She glanced back at her clutch.

"It'll be fine. Levi will keep an eye on it."

She looked at the sandy-haired cowboy who was gazing toward the door, completely oblivious to anything on the table.

"Uh-huh." Sarcasm dripped from her tone.

Dance's hand moved to the small of her back to guide her. "Trust me, no one will disturb it. This is Chapel Pines." Mild pride lingered in his voice. Small town values. What would it be like to live in a place where you could leave your things unattended in a bar? Besides, Levi was there.

Dance guided them through the moving circle of couples to the smaller circle of dancers in the middle. "Beginners take the center." He leaned in close to be heard over the music.

"Don't want us messing up the rhythm of the more advanced?" She grinned up at him.

"That's right. Ever done the Two-Step before?"

"No. Never."

"All right, we'll take it slow." He took her right hand into his left and positioned their arms out to the side. His right hand curved onto her shoulder. "Put your left arm on mine and hold onto my bicep."

"Like this?" She lay her hand over the bulge of muscle beneath his plaid shirt. It was a nice bicep. She tried to not appreciate it so much.

"Perfect." He grinned. "Now we're going to just glide right in with it. Go back with your right. Ready?"

Constance nodded, eager to give it a go. On the

next beat they were off, moving with the inside circle of couples. It only took a few stumbles before she settled into the gliding rhythm. His scuffed boots looked large next to her high heels.

He chuckled. "Look up."

She glanced up. "What?"

His lips turned down in a fleeting frown that looked like the equivalent of an indulgent eye roll. "Stop watching our feet. You have this."

"Okay." She took another quick glance down, stumbled a step and then looked back up. Her eyes met Dance's and she was immediately drawn into the steadiness of his gaze. She stumbled again, her foot colliding with his.

He tugged her closer and Constance's core temperature decided to kick up a few degrees.

"Okay?" Dance's voice husked close to her ear.

"Uh-huh." She nodded dumbly. The press of people on the dance floor sure were putting out a lot of heat.

His hand was a pleasant weight on

her shoulder. "You're doing great. Just keep your head up and trust me to steer you around. I won't let you run into anyone. Promise."

"All right. I trust you." And she did. Constance blinked at the notion of trusting a relative stranger so quickly. There was just something about him. Sturdy. Protective. He reminded her of her grandmother's Irish wolf hound Sarge. The beast followed Nana around like her personal Secret Service Agent. Sarge was large, patient, and loyal to a fault. Constance grinned about what Dance would think of being compared to a dog. "Your name wouldn't happen to be Sarge?"

"What? No. Eyes on me." He smiled. His fingers slid up to the back of her neck.

"Hogarth?"

"Hogarth?" He grimaced.

"Cody?"

"What's wrong with Cody?"

"Nothing. I just don't like it. There was a Cody in second grade who was mean to me."

His brows drew sternly down over eyes that were…amused. What had her mom once said of her father? He had laughing eyes. "It's not Cody, is it?"

"No."

"Good. I would've hated to have to hate your name."

"Reserve judgement." Those laughing eyes glimmered. "You don't know what it is."

"Eyes on me." He smiled. His fingers slid up to the back of her neck.

They made it around the inner circle a few times without a hiccup. Constance was feeling rather proud of herself. Two-Stepping wasn't too hard. "This is fun."

"Up for a spin?"

"Yes!"

She barely got the word out when she was turned about on the four beats and was back in Dance's arms, closer than before and picking right up where they left off. It was exhilarating, moving together nearly as one.

The song morphed into another, and they continued dancing.

He took her into several more turns and an open side-to-side kind of position with their hands crossed. Somehow, he had maneuvered them into the outer circle where they coasted along with all the other couples.

It was the most fun she'd had in…well, she wasn't sure how long. Formal dinners and stuffy events didn't hold a candle to kicking her heels up and letting loose.

Grinning widely, she glanced up and found him staring at her with an expression similar to an artist studying a painting he wasn't quite sure what to make of.

Heat flushed across her skin. She immediately dropped her gaze from his intent eyes to his jaw and kept her focus there. Much safer. She tried to explain away the reactions she was having to him looking at her that way. She had no business having any reaction. Except that it was a really nice jaw. Firm. It jutted out a little too. There was a tiny mole or freckle just beneath the left corner of his lip.

Her eyes lifted fractionally to take in those lips, and…what was wrong with her? She was engaged. Her heart plummeted to her stomach. Her finger twitched on his bicep; Marcus's engagement ring felt suddenly very heavy.

Marcus abandoned her on their wedding day. They weren't married. They were no longer engaged. Why was she still wearing his ring?

She missed a step. Her leg twisted against Dance's.

She should have gone down, but Dance somehow kept her up and just about lifted her off her feet and kept going, steering them off the floor.

The couple coming up behind them expertly quick-stepped to the side to avoid them.

"You all right?" His hands remained firmly on her. "You look kind of flushed."

"I'm fine. I just—" Her face heated. She

was not going to let Marcus spoil everything. This was her honeymoon, darn it. She was going to have a good time. "Let's keep dancing." She tugged on his arm.

The man didn't budge an inch. Instead, he pulled her the other way. "In a minute, Ginger Rogers. How about sitting the next one out in favor of wetting our whistles?"

Taking her hand again, he led her back through the crowd to their table. Sure enough, her clutch was still there.

As was Levi, a frown etched into his forehead. He stood as they approached, seating himself again once Constance was in her chair. A gal could definitely get used to the charm of southern gentlemen.

She smiled at him. "Have you gone out on the floor yet?" She tried to engage him in small talk. He had guarded her purse after all.

He tipped his head. "Not much for dancing." His attention strayed toward the entrance. He wasn't much for joining a conversation either. He'd be a challenge, this one, but Constance knew she could get more than a sentence at a time out of him.

"Well, the Two-Step is now officially my favorite dance." She followed his gaze toward the door. "Are you waiting for someone?"

"No, ma'am."

Sure seemed like it. She let it drop. "So, what do you do for work then?" She decided to move to a safer subject.

"Carpentry."

"Levi is working on the carriage house up at the inn," Dance added. He took a swallow of beer and Constance stared at the way his Adam's apple moved in his strong throat column.

She blinked. What the heck was wrong with her? She was only a day away from having been dumped. She'd never looked at Marcus's Adam's apple in this state of fascination.

Her heart thudded at that realization. In a near panic, she searched her brain for something about Marcus that had beguiled her. Um, um, his straight, thin nose? It was nice, yet...kind of weak really. As was his chin now that she thought about it.

Oh crap. Something good. She was searching for something good. His hands. Nice long fingers. He kept them clean and manicured. And they were soft.

She glanced at Dance's hands, at the length of his fingers, definitely not manicured. She shivered at the callused feel of them on the back of her neck when they were dancing...

She was a terrible, terrible person. Where was her loyalty to the man she'd just about married?

Swallowing hard, she turned her attention back to Levi and safety.

"Really? That's you working in the carriage house? I noticed that you're salvaging most of the original pieces. Are you going to keep the shiplap boards?" She was rambling like a loon. "What are your plans for separating the space into rooms?"

Levi looked to Dance in obvious desperation for his friend to save him from her ambush of questions. Dance simply sat back and rested his elbows on the arms of his chair.

She tried to ignore him, tried to not turn her head to face him, even as his presence was a magnetic pull on her peripheral. Levi. Keep her gaze on Levi. "Have you gone through everything in there? Dance and I found the most amazing antique box. I'd love to know exactly where in the carriage house you found it."

"A box?" Levi shook his head.

"Yes, about this big." Constance measured about a foot wide space between her hands.

Levi scrunched his forehead. "I don't remember any box." He scooted his chair back from the table and grabbed up the empty pitcher. "I'm going to go see about a refill." He practically bolted in his retreat.

Constance put her elbows on the table and rested her chin on her hand. "I scared him away, didn't I?

"Like a fox from a farmer." Dance's eyes glimmered with amusement.

"I was just trying to be friendly. I'm usually pretty good at making people feel comfortable."

"I can see that."

She narrowed her eyes, detecting the hint of sarcasm.

"I am. Ask anyone."

"I didn't say you weren't."

"Well, okay then." She stuck out her lips, enjoying the banter between them. It was friendly because they were friendly. Just two friendly people having fun.

"I get the feeling your friend Levi wasn't dancing because who he wants to dance with isn't here."

Dance had his beer halfway to his mouth and stopped. His gaze slid sideways. "How do you figure?"

"From the way he keeps looking toward the

door. Does he have someone?"

"No," Dance answered a little too quickly. Oh, there was a story behind that all right. And she was perpetually nosey enough to want to know what it was.

"You're certain of that?" She took a sip of her water.

"He doesn't have a gal."

Dance's eyes narrowed. His expression was too hard to read. "Why? You interested?"

Constance nearly choked on her water. "Gosh, no!" She glanced at her ring. "Technically, I'm on my honeymoon."

Dru flounced into the chair next to Constance before Dance made it to his feet.

"Sit down, dreamboat, before you pull a muscle." Dru fanned herself with her hand. "Whew, that was fun. These cowboys are scrumptious."

The red head she had been dancing with came up behind her with a large thin crust pizza.

"You set that right here in front of me, sweetie. I'm starving."

The smell set Constance's mouth to watering.

"Dancing will do that to you." The guy sat beside Dru, and they both reached for the same slice. He let her have the slice and she winked at him.

"More than just dancing whets my appetite." Dru let her arm rest against his.

His face reddened enough that his freckles nearly disappeared.

Constance groaned quietly at the line and Dru tapped the side of her foot under the table, her meaning clear: Watch and learn. The master of flirtations was beginning her heart-breaking tour across Texas. Dru had turned it into an art form. Poor guy.

Constance nibbled on her pizza. She felt Dance's gaze on her and tried not to flush.

He stood and held his hand out to her. "Ready for another spin on the floor?"

Butterflies fluttered in her stomach. The effect he had on her was unnerving. Against her better judgement, she took his hand.

"Melvin, right?"

"What?"

"Your real name."

"No. Definitely not Melvin."

"Harold?"

Back at the McCagan, Constance brushed her teeth in a tired daze. She was both exhausted and exhilarated. She couldn't remember when she and Marcus had such an enjoyable time. Had to have been before they'd gotten engaged six months ago. After that their relationship had turned into a routine of business dinners and events for his advertising firm, or bridal venues with her mother.

When had they lost the fun and

spontaneity in their relationship? Had it ever really been there?

Is that why Marcus stood her up at the altar? He realized something important between them just wasn't there before she did?

She twisted the engagement ring around her finger. Marcus had the wedding band that went with it.

She supposed she should return it. She pulled the ring off and stared at it. She'd worn it so proudly, stared at it so much, that her finger felt naked without it.

Yet…the feelings of sadness and finality she expected didn't come. She felt…nothing really. Constance frowned and rinsed her mouth of the toothpaste. There really was something not right about her. She'd planned on marrying Marcus for half a year. Shouldn't she feel something?

Anger even? Resentment maybe? Hurt that he left her so easily?

She set the ring on the counter with a subtle

clink on the porcelain.

The diamond glittered in the florescent light. It was a beautiful ring. The ceremony and reception had been planned to be stunning. She felt like a princess in her gown.

But now that those things were gone, that Marcus was gone—her chest pinched a little. She swallowed hard. Because all she felt was relief.

FIVE

THE LAPPING water on the lakeshore soothed Constance as she and her friends soaked in the Texas warmth on the lounge chairs. Children laughed and splashed in the water, watched by the two lifeguards on duty and their parents. The air smelled of wild grasses and sunscreen.

"You danced with that red head the entire night," Annette accused Dru. "That's a first for you, isn't it?"

"What do you mean?" White-framed sunglasses on, Dru smiled demurely.

"One guy an entire night when there were plenty to dance with." Beth pushed up on an elbow.

"Austin's funny and a good dancer. I was enjoying myself so there was no reason to swap out. What I want to know…" Dru pulled her sunglasses down to give Constance the sharp eye. "What is going on with you and Mr. Yummy?"

"Nothing." Constance blinked. "He's funny and a good dancer, too."

"Uh-huh." All three women said at once and then started laughing.

"You had googly eyes all night," Annette pointed out.

"Admit it, you like him," Beth said.

Constance sighed and sat up. "I do like him, more than I should in my current situation. Maybe this is just rebound attraction?" A girl could hope. "I don't know. I've never been on the rebound before."

Dru pushed her sunglasses up and turned her face to the sun. "So, what if it is? You deserve a rebound fling."

"I'd say," Annette chimed in.

Constance scrunched her nose. "It just feels…disloyal somehow."

All three of her friends pushed up on their elbows to stare at her.

Dru snorted. "Disloyal? To Marcus? Honey, he left you on your wedding day."

"Didn't have the guts to say anything before then," Beth agreed. "You don't owe him a thing."

Dru took her sunglasses completely off to make her point. "More than anyone I know, you deserve to have a little fun, a little harmless flirtation with a dreamy Texan."

Constance looked down at her naked ring finger. A little harmless flirtation. That didn't sound so awful put that way. And she did enjoy Dance's company. "Yeah, yes, I guess I do."

"That's my girl." Dru settled back down and closed her eyes.

"So…" Beth smiled up into the sunlight.

"How are we going to set up more alone time for Constance with that good looking man?"

Constance frowned because that was a valid question.

After lunch, Constance went straight to the lobby with her friends' encouragement trailing after her. What an odd honeymoon this turned out to be with her bridesmaids urging her to seek out the company of a guy who wasn't her fiancé, er, husband—ex-fiancé. Definitely ex.

She briefly wondered where Marcus had gone. Was he holed up in his penthouse? Or had he taken off to parts unknown to hide out, leaving her to deal with the fallout?

A flash of anger brushed through her veins. What an inconsiderate coward.

Darn it. She didn't want to think about him.

She didn't want anything to sour her mood. She was going to put Marcus behind her and enjoy herself. There was nothing wrong with that.

Besides, she'd bet a dollar to donuts that Dance wouldn't stand a lady up. Ever.

Her hand paused midway to the manager's office door. Maybe she shouldn't do this.

Her heart thumped in anticipation at seeing him around. He had been scarce since last night. Not that she had been looking for him. The logical place to find him was the office since he had to be upper management...unless he had the day off. Which, if that was the case, she was a little disappointed that he hadn't sought her out. Maybe last night he was just being an attentive employee to the inn's heartbroken guest. Everyone at the McCagan had to know about her circumstances by now.

Why would she ever think he wanted to spend his free time with someone her supposed groom didn't even want?

She dropped her hand when the door swung open.

"Oh." Shannon blinked at her, although the woman recovered quickly. "Miss Chambers. Can I help you?"

"Um, actually..." She peered into the room behind the woman to see if anyone else was in there. "I'm, um, curious about something. Do you have a few minutes?"

"Of course. Is there a problem?"

"Oh no, no problems. Everything is wonderful. Your staff has been great. It's just...well, back home I run *Antique Treasures.*"

"Really? That's your company? I've bought a few pieces from there." Her smile brightened.

Pride warmed Constance's heart that Shannon had heard of her little boutique. She took great care in picking and authenticating every piece herself.

"That's kind of what I wanted to talk to you about."

"Antiques?" Shannon's nose scrunched. "I don't

understand, but please, come in." She stepped back inside the office and let Constance follow her in.

Constance took the same seat she had the day before. She didn't see the old box anywhere. "First, I have a confession to make."

"Oh?" Shannon sat opposite her across the desk.

"I have a habit of going into places I shouldn't. And, well, that carriage house of yours out back was just begging to be explored." She paused to gauge Shannon's reaction to her breaking and entering. If anything, the woman appeared amused.

"It's beautiful in there," Constance quickly went on. "The character of the building is amazing. The potential of what you can do with that place has my imagination going a million different ways. I'll have to come back when it's finished." Even as she said it, she knew she was coming back.

Shannon's lips curled. Constance could tell it wasn't prideful, but more of a softening in her expression, springing from her heart. The carriage house meant more than just extra revenue to the inn's owner.

"Thank you, but what does our carriage house have to do with your company?"

"I found something of interest in there. I know the carriage house is off-limits to guests, but I went in anyway and there was this old box piled in with stuff I assume is meant to be sorted through…and well, I just couldn't help myself."

Shannon chuckled quietly. "Don't tell me that inside the box you found the gold ingots of the Lost Padre mine?"

"The what?"

Shannon shook her head, clearly messing with her and Constance grinned.

"No, but almost as good. An exquisite antique tortoiseshell comb, hand carved if I'm not mistaken. It looks to be from around the late eighteen hundreds. I'd like to authenticate it with your permission. Without any fee, of course. But if you do decide to sell it, I'd like to make a bid to purchase it myself. But either way, I'm dying to know the story behind it. Besides, it will take my mind off...well, you know. You'd be doing me a favor."

Shannon's eyes widened incrementally as Constance spoke. "An antique comb? It was out in the carriage house?"

"Yes. It must have been tucked safely away, maybe hidden or fallen between the shiplap boards and the interior wall until your workmen uncovered it and stuck it in one of the piles."

"That's pretty amazing. I wonder how it got to be there?" Her eyes grew dreamy, and Constance sensed a kindred enthusiast. "How would you go about authenticating it?"

"That's the best part. There was a letter inside written to an Ady from a woman named Peg. Do you know who either of them could be?"

Shannon shook her head. "You got me."

"Well, that's our best clue, so the first step

is to find out who they were and then go from there. So, is that a go-ahead?" Constance waited with anticipation. She was more into figuring out the mystery of the comb than she'd thought.

"Yes, that's a go-ahead." Shannon smiled. "Where is the comb? Do you have it in your suite?"

"Gosh no, I wouldn't have just taken it." She glanced around the cozy office again. "I thought it'd still be in here." She'd hoped to find Dance in here too. "We brought it in from the carriage house."

"We?"

"One of your employees caught me out there and we brought it in here together." She didn't want to get Dance in trouble.

Shannon didn't seem fazed that one of her employees used the office. "Which one?"

She guessed it was okay then. "Dance." She realized she hadn't asked for his last name.

Shannon's gaze jerked up. "He told you he's an employee?"

Constance's heart jolted inside her chest. "He's

not? But you asked him to show my friends to the suite. I thought…"

"Relax." Shannon's eyes sparkled. "He's my brother."

Constance slouched back in her chair as the new information caught up to her. "So, he does work here."

"If you can call what he does here as work." Shannon grinned then shook her head. "Actually, I'm teasing. Dance takes running the inn very seriously. Sometimes too seriously if you ask me. He works harder than any of us." Shannon got out of her chair and started going through the cabinets beneath the credenza. "He must have put the box in here somewhere."

Constance scooted to the edge of her seat, stretching her neck to better see. She wanted to help look, but thought it'd be rude to go through a business's drawers. Then a thought struck her. "So, what's your brother's real name?"

"Oh no you don't." Shannon didn't stop

to glance at her. "Last time I gave that away, my best doll's head was used for batting practice."

"He didn't."

"He did and said the two weeks of mucking out manure was worth it."

"His name is that bad?"

Shannon did look at her, her features stilling in contemplation before she shrugged. "I think it suits him, but what do I know? I'm his sister and see him differently."

Constance grinned, liking Shannon more and more. She definitely enjoyed the glimpse of what having a sibling was like.

"Is it in there?" Standing, Constance leaned over the desk to better see.

The door swung open. Shannon twisted around. "Well speak of the devil".

SIX

DANCE had been thinking of Constance all morning. That wasn't entirely true. He'd dreamed about her last night too, all creamy skin and curves, sunflower hair and those huge expressive eyes.

He had no business thinking of a woman, who was barely a day jilted in the way he was thinking about her.

Opening the door to his office and finding her pretty derriere in perfect view as she leaned over the desk was not going to do a blasted thing to rein in his wayward thoughts.

"Well speak of the devil," Shannon said. An eyebrow lifted in sync with the turning down of one corner of her lip as if she knew all too well where his gaze had been lingering.

Caught, Dance played nonchalant.

Constance turned to smile at him. "Hi," she said almost shyly.

"Hi." He was being such a girl, but finding Constance here was like scoring an extra toy in the claw machine.

"Barnibus?" she immediately asked.

"Not even close. What's going on?"

"We're looking for the tortoiseshell comb," Constance told him, imagining him as a Barnibus. Nope, didn't fit at all. Barney? Nada on that too.

"In the wrong place." He stepped in and took the box down from the top of the bookshelf and set it down on the desk.

Shannon put her hands on her hips. "I never would have found it there, though I should have known."

Dance tapped her on the top of her head. "I can't help it if you missed your growth spurt."

Shannon went for his ribs and pinched.

"Ouch." He went back around to the other side of the desk for safety and settled on the arm of the chair Constance occupied. He'd done it without thinking about how familiar a position it was, but it had felt natural and now it would be awkward to move. Even if he wanted to. Which he didn't.

She smelled nice. Some blossomy kind of fragrance, not too strong. He wondered if it was the shampoo they supplied at the inn and decided then and there that they would forever be ordering from that supplier.

Thankfully Shannon didn't say anything about where he sat, though going by the twitch of her mouth she wanted to. Out of respect for their guest, she'd stay quiet. For now. He most certainly could look forward to a lecture about relationships with guests later.

Then again, she was the one who had first suggested he and his friends hang around as eye candy.

Constance's attention was fully on the box. "May I?"

"Absolutely." Shannon gave Dance another pointed look before she leaned forward, her face suffused with curiosity and a lightness he hadn't seen on her for months. "The box really doesn't look like much. I'm not surprised Levi set it aside. You do have a talent for recognizing possibilities, Miss Chambers."

Constance glanced up. "Thank you." She turned the box, so the opening faced Shannon and lifted the lid.

"Oh," Shannon cooed. "It's stunning."

Dance had to admit he enjoyed seeing his sister's look of awe. Beside him, Constance was beaming.

"Is it safe to handle it?" Shannon asked.

"The comb is, but wear gloves to handle the letter." Constance smiled. She really did love this stuff. "It's incredible, full of heartbreak."

"Do we have gloves? I'd really love to see it."

Shannon looked to Dance. That was his clue to get out the first aid kit again and unfortunately move away from Constance.

Shannon lifted the comb from the velvet. Her head cocked to the side. "I've seen this before."

"You have?" Dance and Constance said in unison and then looked at each other.

Dance turned away first. "When?" He set the first aid kit on the desk beside the box.

Shannon ran a finger along the curved edge of the comb. "Well, not the real thing, but I'm sure I've seen a picture of it in one of Granny's old albums."

"Really? That might tell us who Peg and Ady are. Can I see them?" Constance slipped the gloves on to take the folded letter out of the lid.

"They're at the house. I'll get them after I pick Brighton up from preschool and meet you later."

"I can pick them up," Dance volunteered. His gaze slid toward Constance. "We could go together."

"You'd never find the right album I think

it's in."

Disappointment dragged his mood down. Dance rubbed the back of his neck. This was stupid. If he wanted to spend more time with Constance, he should simply ask her out. And not on the pretext of taking her entire bridal party out for fun like before. But it was too soon. Not for him, because forget her fiancé. The guy was an idiot for letting someone as amazing as Constance go like that. But it had to be too soon for her. She was going to marry the guy two days ago for hollerin-out-loud.

Dance was not the kind of guy to take advantage of a heartbroken woman at her most vulnerable.

"Tell you what." Shannon slipped on a glove as well. "Wyatt's covering the inn tonight. Why don't you bring Constance over for supper and we'll go through the album together?"

"Oh, I couldn't impose," Constance hedged.

"Nonsense," Shannon cut her off. "I'll grab

something from our kitchen here so there won't be any imposition. Besides, I'd love some grown-up company for a change of pace."

"I'm grown-up company," Dance defended himself.

Shannon rolled her eyes and deadpanned to Constance. "Isn't he cute?"

Dance huffed, but all was forgiven when Constance agreed to dinner. "In that case, I'd love to." She grinned.

Dance's spine unbuckled. *Thank you, Shannon.*

Constance and Shannon immediately turned their attention to the letter, which was good since Dance couldn't keep the contentment off his face. Constance most likely wouldn't recognize it for what it was, but Shannon knew him too well. He even allowed himself a small smile as the two women awed and sighed over the content on the yellowed paper. Oh no, tears welled in Shannon's eyes.

Without saying anything, Constance

handed Shannon a tissue, and then looked up at him. "Is your name Herbert? Herbert seems like a fitting name for an innkeeper."

Off-guard for a second, Dance stayed silent. Shannon glanced up at him with amusement. At least her eyes were no longer shimmering. Constance's distraction had done the trick.

"No." He went along with her. "It's not Herbert."

"Why didn't you tell me you me you were one of *the* McCagans?"

"I didn't *not* tell you."

"You let me believe you were an employee."

"You were snooping in our carriage house and then you broke my nose," he shot back. "And technically, I do work for the inn."

She eyed him narrowly. "You told me it wasn't broken."

"It isn't."

"Well, then, I guess we're even."

"How do you figure that?"

"You didn't tell me who you were, and I didn't break your nose."

"How does that...?" He tried to follow her logic and failed. Because it wasn't a clear path. He gave up, and shook his head. "Nevermind. Since I am a McCagan, I do have work to do." Except it was his day off, but she didn't know that. He wasn't really sure why he'd come in anyway. "I'll see you both tonight. Constance, I'll pick you up at six. " With that, he left the office before she could make other arrangements, and headed toward his mom's room. Yes, that's why he had come, to check on his mom. A certain curious blonde had nothing to do with it.

The moment Constance stepped out of the office, her phone rang. Fishing the cell out of her pocket, she frowned at the screen. Her mother. She let it ring again. She wasn't ready for this.

Dru had run interference with her mother when Beth and Annette whisked her away after the disaster of the wedding-that-wasn't and since then she'd let all her calls go to voicemail. Constance sighed. She couldn't avoid her mom forever.

"Hello." She held the phone to her ear and walked across the foyer to get outside.

"Constance. Finally. I've called at least a hundred times."

Suddenly the air inside the inn was cloying. "I know. I'm sorry. I just needed some time." Constance pulled open the door.

"You needed some time?" Her mother's heels clicking on the slate tiles of her townhouse echoed through the phone. "Meanwhile I've been left here to deal with the embarrassment and questions. Questions that I don't have the answers to."

"I'm sorry. I didn't mean to put you in that spot. I didn't mean for any of this to happen."

"Then why did it? What did you say to him?"

"Nothing." Constance sighed. "I don't know why Marcus took off." She just wasn't enough for Marcus. He didn't want her. "Why don't you go out of town for a few days? Stay with Aunt Lil." Constance ran down the steps, past the parking lot and headed across the lawn.

"Nonsense. Someone has to be here to speak with the reporters."

"Reporters? How is this newsworthy? How would they even…?" She stopped in the grass. "You called the paper?"

"Of course I did. A Wentworth leaves his bride at the altar, everyone wants to know the details and who better to get them from than the distraught mother of the poor jilted bride?"

"You don't sound distraught," Constance said dryly and picked up her pace as though she could outwalk this entire conversation.

"Don't be flippant. I'm devastated."

"Yet I was the one left standing there holding the bouquet. By the way, Mom, I'm fine."

"Of course you are, dear. You're a Chambers. We're made of stern material. Now tell me, did Marcus give you any indication that he was getting cold feet? Did you two have a fight? Did you say anything that might have driven him away?"

Constance nearly dropped the phone. Anger and hurt tightened inside her chest like a vise. "No, I didn't say anything."

Oblivious, her mom went on. "You had to have done something. He was the perfect match. You two were so wonderful together."

"Apparently we weren't."

"Has he tried to reach you at all?"

"No. And he's not going to."

"How do you know if you've been avoiding all your calls?"

"Mom, trust me. He's not going to call." If he did, would she take it?

"You never know. Young men these days can be fickle." Her mother sounded so hopeful; Constance didn't have the desire to crush it. After all, it had been her mom's dream wedding as much as hers, her way of vicariously having the big extravaganza she'd been denied when she eloped with a poor college professor against her parents' better judgement. Her dad didn't even teach at an Ivy League university. Constance couldn't really blame her mom for wanting the big wedding she couldn't have herself.

"All I'm saying is to keep your phone with you," her mother continued. "You never know. Poor Marcus is probably beside himself."

Poor Marcus. Constance rolled her eyes and told her mom what she wanted to hear. "Okay. I will."

There was a pause. "Constance? I know you think I'm heavy handed sometimes, but everything I do is for your good. Trust me on this. Now, how are you holding up?"

All the stiffness melted from Constance's spine. Her eyes teared up and her throat clogged. "I'm good. Really."

"That's my daughter. We'll weather through this."

"Thanks, Mom." Her voice was thick, betraying more emotion than she was comfortable with. "I have to go. Talk to you soon?"

"Hold your chin up high, honey."

"I will."

She ended the call, feeling both gloomy and somewhat sensitive. Her mom loved her. She knew that, but she'd been so excited about the prospects of getting back in what she thought of as society's good graces, and showing her own parents that her daughter was marrying into the upper crust, that Constance sometimes felt like that took precedence over what she wanted. She'd let her mom have full rein over the wedding planning. And it hurt more than she could say that her own mother thought that somehow Marcus calling it off was her fault.

Maybe it was. She thought back to the latest conversations between them. Marcus had seemed distracted, not really interested in the details of their wedding, but he never had been, leaving it all up to her, or more to the point, her mother. Should his lack of interest in the wedding have been a sign that he was losing interest in her as well?

The whir of an approaching vehicle yanked her out of her musings. A glossy black golf cart with a mean-looking rack of longhorn horns mounted above the headlights came barreling toward her over the lumpy grassland and stopped with a skid of dirt flying up as the cart slipped sideways. *Madelaine Winery* was emblazoned in gold along the side panel.

Instinctively, she hopped out of the way at the same time a tall lanky old cowboy unfolded from behind the wheel. Hands on hips, bolero tie, pressed white shirt tucked into neat dark jeans. Silver blue eyes regarded her. Holy petunias, she'd almost been run over by Jock Ewing.

"Ma'am." Even his twang rumbled with authority. "You're about twenty feet onto private property."

"I am?" She looked around. She had long since left the manicured lawn and walked into the untamed meadow between the inn and the neighboring winery. Rows of pretty grapevines were about thirty feet ahead and she would have walked right into them. "Sorry." She ducked her gaze sheepishly. "I was distracted. On the phone. With my mom." She really didn't mean to add that, but she felt like a schoolgirl caught by one of her teachers. "I'll, um, head back."

The man chuckled. "Get in, I'll take you back. I was heading that way anyway."

"Oh, that's okay."

"I wasn't asking. A young filly gets lost on my property, it's my job to get her back where she belongs."

"I wasn't lost. The inn's right over there." She pointed behind them.

Silver gray eyebrows rose above eyes that weren't accustomed to having to ask twice.

"On second thought…" Constance slipped

around the longhorns and slid onto the passenger seat. "I'd love a ride."

His expression didn't budge an inch. He simply bent into the driver's seat and off they went across the bumpy meadow.

"You said I was on your property. You're Mr. Larie, the owner of the winery?"

His countenance did change at that. The corner of his lip curved up. "Yep, though I'd say the winery owns me more than I own her. Bought the first acre of land when I was wet behind the ears."

"That's impressive. I had some of your Chardonnay at the inn. The balance between oak and pear was amazing."

He looked at her out of the corner of his eye. "You know your wines."

Constance grinned. "Only enough to get me into trouble. I actually heard that line used by a wedding planner. But I do know it was the best I've ever had, and the hint of pear was just right."

His eyes creased around the corners.

His mouth pulled up in a pleased smile." That was my Maddie's doing, God rest her soul. She had a way with the grapes. She taught me to walk up and down every row, tasting and watching. I still do. There's no other way to know when the grapes are ready." His voice tapered off.

"I'm sorry, I didn't mean to…"

"Nonsense. She went on ahead of me these last nineteen years, but we had a heck of a life together." His profile softened, completely changing his intimidating presence to that of an old teddy bear.

Constance's throat felt suddenly thick, realizing that she'd never caught that kind of expression on Marcus toward her when he thought she wasn't looking.

"So, what had you so distracted you lost track of where you were?"

"I was talking with my mom, and…" She turned sideways in the seat to face him, hanging onto the canopy frame as they bounced over the uneven ground. "You've been married. And you're a man. Is there something off-putting about me?"

He sputtered and braked the flashy cart to a stop.

Constance winced. "Too much? I'm sorry. I don't know why I just blurt out things I shouldn't to perfect strangers yet have the hardest time expressing how I feel to my own mom."

"I won't fib young lady, you did catch me off-guard. However, I did ask. Now what's this all about then?"

Constance frowned, feeling a little shy now that Mr. Larie was facing her. She took a breath. "My mother thinks I did something to drive away my fiancé."

"So, you're the bride that was left standing at the altar?"

The breath she'd just taken whooshed out. "You know about that?"

"Small county. Anything with half an ounce of amusement is going to get around."

"So glad I could give the entire county something to talk about." She sat back in the seat and folded her arms.

Mr. Larie chuckled. "Now about you doing something to run the fella off, I can't say. Maybe you did, maybe you didn't. But if the man really loved you, nothing you did could have driven him away. If he's a runner, you're blessed to be shut of him early on before you attempted a life together. But I'll tell you this, around these parts, any man who would wait until the day of the nuptials to break it off, well, to my way of thinking, that isn't a man at all. If I was your daddy, I'd be getting out my rifle."

It was an absurd thing to envision Mr. Larie chasing Marcus with his rifle, but for some undefinable reason, it was exactly what she needed to hear. Her heart melted.

"My daddy died when I was fourteen," she said softly, again wondering why she was so bad at just saying whatever came to her mind.

"In that case, if that coward ever shows his face around here, you give me a call and I'll come running."

Constance's eyes widened, staring at him to gauge his seriousness when he cracked a grin and all at once they were laughing together.

After the phone call with her mom, Mr. Larie was just what she needed.

Still chuckling, he put the cart back into gear. "Let's get you back."

SEVEN

DANCE had gotten ambushed in the kitchen by Melodee, panicked as their largest oven wouldn't heat up. It was the oldest oven in the kitchen, had been repaired a dozen times and should rightly be put to pasture out where old appliances live out the remainder of their days, but it was Melodee's favorite and she wouldn't see it go. The redheaded cook leaned anxiously over him while he worked. An hour and a few heating coils later, Dance made his way into the sunroom.

Cletus Larie sat on the wicker loveseat beside Dance's mom in her rocker. From the way their faces were angled away from each other, and both wore rigid frowns, their visit wasn't going so well.

Dance walked into the sunroom and crouched in front of his mother. "Hey Beautiful."

She rolled her eyes.

"Want to go for a walk?"

"No." She turned her head away.

"You need to. The doctor said it will help you recover."

"What d-does he know?" She crossed her arms. "Has he ever had—had a stroke?"

"Not to my knowledge. But I gather he didn't just pull that advice how of a hat either."

"Tired."

"Mom." Dance glanced at Mr. Larie. "Cletus came all the way over just to go for a walk with you."

"Should have…saved…himself the trouble."

"Fine. Then walk with me."

Her eyes flashed to his, flushed with anxiety. It broke his heart to see it. "We'll stay in here," he offered.

Cletus got up and went to the archway and leaned against the doorframe, giving them some space.

His mom still wasn't budging.

Dance sighed, changing tactics. "I've got about an hour. If we take a short walk, I'll read to you." She had a dozen books on audio that Shannon had downloaded for her, but their mom loved being read to by her children. It had been a bedtime treat when they were young, all gathered together and impatient for their turn.

She stomped her feet heavily on the tile and reached out for help to get to her feet. She wasn't happy about it, but by golly, he had gotten her on her feet.

The first few steps went relatively well, even with her one foot turned inward and shuffling. Dance walked slowly, arm supporting her about the waist. They made it across the length of the sunroom when her foot snagged on the other one. She shrieked and nearly went down.

Of course she didn't fall far, barely a few inches as Dance caught her up, steadying her while she got her feet beneath her once more.

"I told you I can't," she grated out.

"You were doing just fine. It was just a little misstep."

"Take me back." She wouldn't look up at him, and he knew they were done. Small victories, he reminded himself. He helped her turn to go back to her rocking chair.

They made it one step, when she jerked to a stop. Her spine straightened into a rigid line.

Cletus stood there, worry creasing his expression. "What happened?" he demanded.

"Nothing." Both Dance and Elise said in unison. She scowled, though pink tinged her cheeks beneath her light skin.

"We're okay here." Dance told Cletus, protective of his mother's embarrassment. Though she had nothing to be embarrassed about. She had gotten up and walked today.

The old vintner's eyes flicked to him, and he nodded, straightening and rolling his shoulders. "Didn't say there was. Simply thought I'd join you." He stepped to the other side of Elise and held out the crook of his elbow.

She pointedly ignored him and started walking back, hanging tightly to Dance.

Cletus gave him an exasperated look over the top of her head. Undeterred, he walked right alongside them the entire slow walk back to the seating area where Dance helped her get comfortable in her rocker. As promised, he picked up the book on the coffee table, frowning at the cover—some kind of fantasy romance. Cletus settled into the opposite chair at the end of the table, making Dance grin. *This should be an interesting read.*

He flipped and began... "She ran to him, across the moor, mist curling at her hips, teasing cloudy swirls around her breech-covered legs until she stood before him, slender hands upon his crisp white shirt."

Constance's friends were more than understanding that she wasn't going to spend the evening with them. They were all crowded into the bridal suite's bathroom.

"The sure way to get over one man is to occupy yourself with another," Dru drolled. Constance squinted, not sure that's what she was doing, or wanted to do. She liked Dance, enjoyed his company. She didn't feel like she was using him to get over Marcus.

"Besides, we have all day together tomorrow," Beth chimed. "There's an amazing antique fair this time of year in a little town called Round Top. It just so happens to be going on this weekend. I've rented a car. The brochure says it's only about two and a half miles once we get past Waco."

"That sounds great," Constance said. What kind of antique dealer hadn't heard of Round Top? It had actually been one of her honeymoon plans with Marcus, but she didn't mention that now. She smoothed down her pencil skirt."

"Besides…" Dru paused to pucker at the mirror to run a smear of lip gloss across her lips. "That handsome brother of his and that shy ginger cowboy are taking us for a tour of the town this evening. We'll be fine without you."

"That outfit's a little too casual." From her perch on the vanity, Annette eyed Constance.

Constance poked a snag of thread back into her yellow sweater, trying to get it back in. "It's supper at his sister's house. We're looking over albums that might hold a clue to that antique comb I told you about. I'm going for casual."

"Oh, I know what will work." Annette went on as though Constance hadn't spoken. "Dru has that little blue number that will be perfect. It's both casual and also says 'hey, I'm an alluring woman'."

"I'll bet," Constance deadpanned.

"Excellent choice." Dru dashed out and in moments came back with a high-waisted dress of pale blue with soft scallops at the sweetheart neckline and hem. It really was more her style than Dru's flashy norm.

"It's for when I want to embrace my girl-next-door vibe." Dru grinned saucily. "Yet somehow I never quite carry it off."

"Because you don't have a girl-next-door vibe," Beth quipped.

They all laughed, even Dru who embraced her nature like no other.

"It's lovely." Constance held the dress up to her.

In minutes she had it on. It fit like it was meant for her. The hem hit just above her knees. On Dru it would have shown much more leg.

"Wow. It doesn't quite have the same effect when I wear it." Dru pursed her glossy lips, studying Constance.

"Thanks, Dru. It's perfect." She hugged her friend. "I can't wait for Dance to see me in this."

Three sets of eyes turned on her in speculation. Beth's gaze narrowed. "So, you do like him."

"I..." Constance shrugged, going for nonchalant. "I never said I didn't. He's sweet."

"Sweet?" Dru grinned.

"He's dreamy," Beth piped in. "All tall and cultured looking like he could have walked off the set of Downton Abbey and then when he speaks all that southern drawl curls your toes." She sighed dreamily.

They all stopped what they were doing to gape at her.

"Maybe you ought to go after him." Dru went back to applying mascara to her lashes. Beth had Jeff back home, so Dru wasn't serious, but Constance's heart took a little dip just the same.

"You should wear your hair up." Annette swooped Constance's hair up on the back of her head. "A simply ponytail I think."

"Oh yes." Dru and Beth agreed, taking the decision out of Constance's hands. In less than twenty minutes they had her styled, make-up on, and shoed, and ushered out the door.

Funny, none of them had ever been as excited to doll her up when Marcus took her out.

EIGHT

HE WAS waiting for her in the lobby, looking every bit what she thought a Texan should look like. Loose distressed jeans over scuffed working man's boots that looked as though they'd seen both hard work and hard play. He had the sleeves of a faded green button-down shirt rolled up and the same black Stetson he wore when they went dancing the other night. He also clutched a small sprig of white daisies.

And he was pacing. He hadn't seen her yet. Constance stopped beside the front desk just to take him in. Beth was right. He was dreamy. And very cute.

He caught sight of her and stopped in

his tracks in the center of the lobby. His eyes swept over her and widened as though what he was seeing put him at a loss for words.

Warmth tingled along Constance's skin. His reaction was better than she'd hoped for, but she hadn't imagined it would make her tongue-tied as well. She never couldn't think of anything to say.

The young man at the check-in desk looked from one to the other and then to Dance again before hiding his grin behind a sheet of paper he picked up.

The movement snapped Dance out of his stupor. He glanced at the front desk and then seemed to mentally shake himself. '

"Hi." He walked over. "You look…" He hesitated as though he wasn't sure he should say the first thing that came to mind, but then went with it anyway. "Beautiful."

Heat crept up Constance's neck and flowed into her cheeks. She licked her lips, feeling suddenly shy.

Dance's gaze zeroed in on her mouth and she swore his Adam's apple bounced. "Here," he croaked, thrusting out the sprig of flowers.

"Thank you." When their fingers brushed, a tiny current of warmth zinged between them. Constance blinked. Dance clasped her hand more tightly. Something indefinable passed across his features.

"Uh..." He seemed to be searching her features. "We should get going. Shannon will be wondering what's keeping us."

He let go of her hand, but only to slide his own to rest at the small of her back as he guided her out the door, which he held open for her, and down the steps to where a valet handed him a set of keys.

She really didn't know what she envisioned him driving, but it hadn't been a rusty open-aired jeep that looked like it dated back to World War II.

"Does that thing actually drive?" She eyed it warily.

Dance's hand paused on the folded

down windshield. "Purrs like a kitten."

"We'll see," she countered as she swiveled into the seat. It didn't have any doors, just lower siding. Dance pulled a thick canvas strap across the empty space of the missing door and clipped it to a hook in the frame.

He didn't blink an eye as he helped her in and then pulled the windshield up, presumably for her comfort, though she believed they were in for a wind-blown drive anyway, before running around the front of the vehicle.

He bent into the old, cracked leather of the driver's seat. "Sorry, I haven't installed seatbelts yet."

Constance stared at the simple console. Round, black-faced circles the center of the instrument panel marked the fuel level, speedometer, water temperature and something else she couldn't quite make out in the faded markings. There were also several levers and knobs she couldn't guess the use for. An old metal sign marked as WILLYS was attached to the small glove box. "How old is this thing?"

"1943 WILLYS." He turned the motor over. It coughed and barked, but then settled into a low murmur. He worked the long stick between them into gear. "My uncle bought it back when I was twelve or so and we restored most of it together." He beamed. The pride in the job they'd done oozed out of him.

A lover of antiques herself, Constance could appreciate his enthusiasm, although she'd never really understood the appeal of the cars. It was the story behind something that intrigued her. Items were always worth more with the proof of its history. And when she couldn't track down the history, she'd sometimes spend hours looking at something and musing about who it once belonged to and what happened to them. She had a fanciful heart, she supposed.

Her stomach bubbled with anticipation over what the McCagan family albums could reveal about the tortoiseshell comb.

They wound their way along the farm-to-market roadway. Dance was a careful driver, avoiding every pothole and easing over most of the largest bumps. Whether to spare the jeep's aged undercarriage or to spare Constance's bottom from the large coils she could feel through the seat, she didn't know. He may drive like a maniac on his own for all she knew. She suddenly realized she wanted to know if that was true about him. She wanted to know a great deal more about him.

Before she knew it they pulled up in front of a cute ranch style house with an amazing wrap-around porch.

Dance parked behind a silver Subaru that must be Shannon's and hustled around the jeep to help her out. Before he gripped the handle, two dark-headed girls shot out of the house and ran down the steps. One was young, about four or five, with bouncing curls and a wooden spoon clutched in her fist. The other looked to be in her late teens or early twenties. The young woman got to Dance first just as he opened the passenger side door.

He'd barely turned when she flew into his arms.

"I missed you!" she exclaimed, hugging him tight around the neck.

Dance chuckled, hugging her back. "You were home less than three weeks ago, silly."

Constance climbed out of the jeep, watching the interaction with interest. Dance's entire demeanor changed around the young woman like a layer of distance he kept between him and everyone else was shed like an outer skin.

"Uncle Dance." The little girl held up the spoon. The end was covered with dough. "We're making cookies." Her impish grin was adorable.

Dance let go of the young woman and bent down, hands on knees. "Cookies? I can't wait to taste them." The girl's dimples came out. Precious. Then her gaze shifted to Constance. "Who's that?"

Dance straightened. "This is Constance.

She's a guest at the inn."

Both girls eyed her like cats sniffing out another who came into the territory.

"Constance," Dance said. "These are Chloe and Brighton, my sister and niece, Shannon's daughter. Chloe's back for the weekend from Baylor University." Pride brightened his features. "Girls, this is Constance."

"Hi." Brighton stared up at her with large dark eyes. "Do you like cookies?"

"I'd have to say yes on that one." Constance gave her answer with the seriousness it deserved.

The little girl's brows furrowed as she considered that. "Do you like to have ice cream with the cookies?"

Oh, she could tell that her answers were on trial here.

"Ice cream is a good choice, especially when the cookies are warm just out of the oven and the ice cream starts to melt over them. Is that how you like to eat your cookies?"

Brighton's eyes widened. "I never did it that way." She looked up at Chloe. "Can we do it like that?"

Chloe smiled. "I think I saw some ice cream in the freezer."

Brighton grabbed Constance's wrist and started pulling her toward the house. Apparently, she'd passed the Brighton cookie test.

Constance glanced back at Dance and smiled. He returned her grin easily, although Chloe's look was more cryptic.

The moment they walked in the door, a delicious aroma hit her. Whatever it was, it set her belly to growling and she realized she was hungrier than she thought.

Shannon was putting aluminum catering pans on the table that was just a few steps from the large island that separated the kitchen from the living area. It was an open design, making the spaces seem larger than they were. It was a great space, both roomy and cozy at the same time.

"Hi, Constance. I see Brighton found you. Just take a seat on the couch. I'll have the rest of this on the table in a moment."

"I can help."

"No." Brighton still had a hold of her. "Make cookies."

Constance looked at Shannon to gauge her thoughts on the matter.

Shannon shrugged. "She's the boss of the cookie operation."

Chloe waltzed into the kitchen after them and ruffled Brighton's curls. "Went and replaced me, have you?"

"No." Brighton climbed up onto the stool that was placed beside the island. "I want you both," she said like the CEO of the house cookie making industry she was. Something within Constance melted at the inclusion. She'd made cookies plenty of times, but always on her own. She couldn't recall being taught by her mother. Baking wasn't exactly a Chambers thing to do.

Constance eyed the large mixing bowl with a mixture of dough already in it. Fine splatters of flour on the counter circled the bowl. "What do we need to do?"

"Put in the chocolate chips." Brighton grabbed the bag of mini mint chocolate chips.

"Okay, I'm going to wash my hands real quick."

Dance sat on one of the stools on the other side of the island. "Sink's right behind you."

Constance turned and fell in love with the rest of the kitchen. It was a little cluttered, the counters could use a little updating, maybe swap out for a dark slate and paint the dark cupboards lighter, but it felt lived in, homey. She could practically feel the memories made by a family seep out of the wood and tile, and the nostalgia she hadn't been a part of made her feel sappy.

She turned on the faucet, eyeing the deep farm sink with appreciation.

"So, Constance." Chloe leaned her hip against the counter next to her, hazel eyes glinting.

"You're the one that got dumped on your wedding day."

NINE

"CHLOE!" Dance and Shannon blurted out almost on top of each other. Constance froze, water running over her soapy hands.

She'd passed Brighton's test, but Chloe's would be a little bit harder. She wouldn't let herself be baited, after all, the girl was obviously concerned about who her brother was bringing to Shannon's home, although Chloe didn't really have to worry about that. They'd only just met. She was here to find out more about the antique comb. She had no designs on her brother.

She shut off the faucet and turned to face Chloe. "Yes, that's me, thank you for the reminder. Towel?"

Chloe reached behind her and grabbed the dish towel hanging on the stove handle and handed it to her.

"Thanks." Constance dried her hands and went back to Brighton who was licking cookie dough off her fingers, sharing a conspiratorial giggle with Dance who also had his finger in his mouth.

"Did you pour the whole bag in?" Chloe asked Brighton.

"Uh-huh."

Chloe gave Dance a why'd-you-let-her-do-that glare.

"Let's eat," Shannon sang out.

"But the cookies—" Brighton pouted.

"Let's finish them after dinner so they'll still be warm enough to melt the ice cream," Constance suggested, which seemed to satisfy Brighton.

Chloe didn't prod her anymore throughout the meal. Constance sat beside Dance, enjoying the brisket brought over from the inn's restaurant. They asked her what Connecticut was like this time of year and what she did for a living, staying tactfully away from her called off wedding.

In turn, they told her about their family. She learned Chloe had a twin who was away on an archeological dig as an intern in Peru.

She grew quiet as she watched them. Dance let his guard down around his sisters, teasing and laughing. His skin crinkled around the edges of his eyes when he laughed.

They were all dark brunettes, Shannon and Brighton a little lighter with brown strands that caught in the lamp light, seeming to move on their own.

4Chloe and Dance resembled one another. There was no mistaking they were siblings, both with strong jawlines and dark intelligent eyes. Where the shared features on Dance were handsome, the feminine version made Chloe drop-dead stunning. Her looks combined with her no-holds-barred personality must have all those college boys tangled in knots. Poor things.

Once everyone had their fill, Constance went with Brighton back into the kitchen to finish the cookies while Shannon showed Dance where the boxes with the older photo albums were.

Chloe pulled a cookie sheet out. "Listen, I'm sorry about what I said before. It was rude."

Constance handed Brighton a spoon with the right amount of dough on it. "It's fine. I get it. He's your brother. You're protective. How can you be sure that I'm not the kind of girl who has to always have a man so latched onto the first guy that came along?"

Brighton looked up between them with curiosity, her hand out for the next scoop of cookie dough.

"I appreciate that." Chloe eyed her over the top of Brighton's curls. "So, are you that kind of girl?"

Constance paused with the next spoonful. "No." Brighton plucked the spoon from her hand and plopped the dough on the baking sheet. "I promise you, Chloe, I have no interest in Dance like that.

I'm not on the rebound. And I like him enough to not do that to him. I don't want to mess anyone up."

Chloe studied her, seeming to look for the truth of that in her features. "Well, your interest might not be the problem."

Constance squinted at her. "What do you mean?"

Chloe lowered her voice. "I know my brother. I see the way he looks at you."

An unexpected pleasure tingled its way through her veins to nestle into her heart. She hoped Chloe couldn't detect any of it coming out as a blush on her cheeks. "I...I don't know what to say to that."

"I don't either," Chloe admitted. "You seem like a good person. Just...just don't hurt my brother."

The last thing Constance would ever want

to do was hurt Dance. As they cleared the coffee table to make room for the photograph albums, Constance worried over what Chloe said.

Maybe Dru's advice about giving herself a chance to heal by flirting with a handsome man wasn't fair to Dance. It had seemed harmless at first, but not if Dance was beginning to have deeper feelings for her like Chloe suspected he did.

Again, that little fissure of pleasure hitched in her heart. Dang it. Who was she kidding? She was beginning to like him more than was good for her too. How was that possible?

She was heartbroken over Marcus, wasn't she?

She stared blankly at the albums laid out in front of her until a picture caught her attention of a family. Parents, two boys and three daughters. It was one of those still black and white tintypes where nobody smiled, probably because they had to remain still for close to a minute for the exposure to appear on the tin place. Except this picture wasn't completely frozen in time. The youngest boy, a toddler, had moved, blurring his face. Which made it a flawed photograph, but to her the flaw created something that much more rich and interesting.

"What's the thing we're looking for?" Chloe sat on the arm of the sofa next to Dance. Constance was between him and Shannon.

"I'll go get it." Shannon got up.

"It's a bridal comb," Constance explained. "It's actually very rare as it's made from tortoiseshell, which isn't used anymore."

"And it was in the carriage house?" Chloe's nose scrunched a bit.

"Levi must have unearthed it without looking into the box it was in." Dance turned the page in the album in his lap.

Chloe blinked. Her cheeks pinkened a little at the mention of Levi. Huh?

"Here it is." Shannon returned and set the box down on top of a closed album and sat back down on the sofa before opening the lid.

Chloe sighed. "Wow. It's exquisite."

Constance leaned forward, once again awed by the beauty.

Brighton got off the plush chair she'd been curled up on to take a look. "Put it on me, Mommy." She reached for it, but Shannon was quicker, grasping the little fingers. "It's very old, honey, and can break easily. We need to keep it safe in the box."

"But it's 'pose to go in the hair," Brighton insisted.

"Yes, and it will." Shannon kissed Brighton's knuckles. "But only on very special occasions."

"But…"

"Hey, kiddo, it smells like the cookies are about done." Chloe saved the day by taking the little girl into the kitchen area.

Constance smiled after them, enjoying the domestic scene they made behind the island counter. She liked Dance's sisters, the comfortable lived-in home. She liked everything about being here. It was like getting a peek into the secret world of siblings, the teasing, the protectiveness, and the genuine affection that surrounded them as a unit.

"I wish I could remember which of these albums the picture is in." Shannon turned a page of old black and whites.

"I hope you didn't imagine seeing the comb in one of these," Dance said, studying a shot of a guy in working man's bib-and-brace overalls. "Look at Uncle George. What a character he was."

Shannon smiled warmly.

Constance caught the shared look between them as they thought of the uncle it was obvious they had been fond of.

They went back to searching their respective albums. Constance turned the page on the one in front of her, drawn to the faces of the McCagans from long ago. A feeling of melancholy came over her like a cold mist. They were a family prone to dark hair and bright eyes going generations back.

Many of the photographs had been taken in front of the inn in various stages of it being built. It hadn't changed much at all once it was finished, unchanging through the decades even as horse drawn carriages in the circle driveway replaced Motel T Fords and then sports cars and Cadillacs. A sense of permanence, tradition, something larger than herself filtered down deep into Constance's bones.

"These would be amazing framed and hung around the lobby of the inn," Constance murmured.

Shannon snapped her head up. "I like that. I like that a lot."

Constance smiled back at her.

"I think this is it," Dance exclaimed.

TEN

DANCE was fairly certain that was the comb. It was fixed on a slight woman posing for her bridal portrait. Her hair was rolled into a thick up-do with the antique comb on the side of her wide bun above a veil that spilled behind her back and one side of her shoulder. By the style of the dress and the faded quality of the picture he thought it might have been taken in the early 1900s.

She stood in the usual pose of the time, straight-backed and unsmiling. Her eyes, however, shone with deep-seated happiness that the rigid posture of the times couldn't extinguish.

He didn't recognize her, nor did she have any of the dark hair and dominant features that had followed the McCagans across the ocean from Ireland.

"Do you know who she is?" Constance leaned closer to him to better see. The scent of soft lilac dusted her skin and it took everything Dance had to keep from leaning in and inhaling deep.

"I don't recognize her." Shannon came around from the other end of the couch to better see and nudged Dance over to give her room. They all shifted over, sandwiching him in much closer proximity as they all wanted to see. Not that he was complaining. Constance's thigh was next to his. The hem of her sundress rode up, giving him an up-close glimpse of thigh and knee. Since he was supposedly looking down at the album anyway, he was able to look his leisure.

"Dance?"

"Hmm?" His attention snapped back to his sister.

"Any idea who this might be?"

"No." He focused once again on the photograph.

The bride in question was a pretty little thing. Slender. Her gown had a high waist with pleats running down the front. Her bouquet was a simple orchid tied with a bow. The veil trailed down her back from where the comb rested near the side of her head. One side of the transparent material was draped in front of her shoulder showing intricate beadwork along the length of the edges. He remembered his mother stitching tiny beads along the sleeves of Shannon's wedding dress. This veil must have taken hours for someone to hand-stitch.

"Look at the detail." Shannon and Constance were oohing and aahing over the early century style of the gown and shoes. Dance's attention kept straying to the bride's face. He was starting to understand Constance's curiosity about the comb. Now that he was looking into the face of the woman who had worn it, his interest in how the comb had come to be lost in their carriage house was growing.

"From the style, I'm pretty sure this was taken around the 1940s." Constance said. "See how her hair was rolled up in front like the Andrews Sisters? Those are called victory rolls. Women in the 40s started wearing their hair longer than they had in the 1920s and 30s and started pinning the front up this way. No one's sure why they called them victory rolls, but the most prominent theory is it had to do with women at home wanting to show their support for the soldiers after World War II began." She ran her finger along the edge of the picture with a look of longing. "Can we take it out and see if anything was written on the back?"

"I don't see why not." Shannon slipped her fingers between the photograph and the black paper of the album page. "There's a bit of old tape or glue here. Ah, got it." She lifted the picture free and flipped it over. Other than the black square of fuzz that came off of the album where the tape was, there wasn't anything written to give them a clue about who the subject of the photograph was.

"Take it to Gramps. See if he knows who she is." Chloe set a couple of plates of ice cream covered cookies on the coffee table between the albums and left again, presumably for more. Brighton was happily eating hers at the counter island, legs kicking back and forth in pure delight.

"Great idea," Shannon said to Chloe as she returned with two more plates and handed one to Dance, keeping the other for herself. She slipped into the overlarge chair with a happy sigh.

"Can you take it over to Grandpa?" Shannon asked Dance.

"Sure." He suspected Shannon was purposefully arranging opportunities for him to spend more time with Constance. Not that he was going to look a gift horse in the mouth. He turned to her, a thread of eagerness tying itself into knots over how he hoped she'd answer. "Want to tag along?"

Her smile was infectious and got Dance's heart to pounding. "If he knows who this bride is, absolutely."

It ended up just being Constance and Beth who made the two- or so-hour drive to Round Top. Both Dru and Annette opted to sleep in after their night on the town with the guys.

Beth was full of enthusiasm for all the treasures they were finding for the shop. Fortunately, the fair had several on-site shippers. Not that they were buying anything large.

Their little shop catered to interior designers. A designer herself, Constance discovered she enjoyed finding just the right pieces and staging them in their shop that inspired other designers to go from there on their own projects. She also consulted when one of her clients got stuck. And Beth was an online genius. Once they expanded to online orders, *Antique Treasures* took off. They'd have to open another shop soon or move to a larger location to house all the items they were able to acquire.

"We should totally think about renting a space here next year," Beth said. "This is huge. We haven't even made it inside the Big Red Barn yet."

"Yeah." Constance lifted a large brimmed Edwardian hat, setting the fluffy ostrich feathers around the brim to floating. "I'd like that."

"And we could wear bikinis to draw in more of a crowd."

"Hmmm-mmmm."

"Okay, what gives?"

"What?"

"You didn't listen to what I just said."

Constance blinked at Beth's tone. The shorter woman had her hands on her hips, staring her down.

"You've been distracted all morning. Nothing distracts you from a good antique hunt. Is it Marcus? You two were coming here, weren't you? I'm sorry. I should have known you would.

I was just so excited—"

"No, Beth, don't think that." Constance stopped her. "That's not it at all."

"So, you and Marcus weren't coming here? And you're not thinking about him?"

"Yes, of course we were. You know me too well." Constance frowned, trying to figure out her own feelings, let alone explain them. "That's just it. I'm not sad that he's not here. I don't miss him at all. Isn't that weird? I know I should be sad, devastated really, but…" She shrugged. "I'm not."

"You're simply numb. In shock over everything." Beth took her arm in hers and they started walking toward the next booth.

"I'm not though." Constance shook her head. "I feel perfectly fine. Marcus did us both a favor. He's smart, successful, good at everything he does."

"That's easy to pull off when everything is handed to you," Beth snarked.

Constance raised a brow, wondering why she'd never heard anything like this before. "Regardless,

I was so enamored with him, I'm not sure we were really in love." She chuckled to herself. "I'm not sure I know what being in love feels like, but it can't be this. If I loved him, I'd be devastated, right?" Her thoughts drifted to the letter they'd found inside the box with the antique comb and her heart trembled. Loss and grief poured from those words, held tightly bound within the parchment for decades. The writing had faded, but the heartfelt plea that Peg had to flee rather than stay among the reminders of her loss resonated across time.

Constance suddenly turned to face Beth. "If Jeff broke up with you today, how would you feel?"

Alarm crossed Beth's features. "He wouldn't. Why are you saying…?"

"Don't worry, I'm not saying he is. Just if he did, how would you feel?"

Crease lines formed over Beth's frown. "Like I was hollow inside. He fills all the parts of me that were empty that I didn't even know needed filling. I'd crawl in a hole and die."

"You wouldn't die." Constance's throat grew thick at her friend's sentiment, wishing with all her heart that she and Marcus had that, but the truth stared her straight in the face. They never had that.

"All right, I wouldn't die, but I'd feel like it." Beth eyed her, searching her features for something that wasn't there, never had been. "You're really okay, then? Your heart is intact?"

"Heart's intact." Constance pushed her arm through Beth's again, feeling somewhat lighter by the admission. She was going to be okay. She would be able to pick up and move on with her life without becoming Mrs. Marcus Wentworth. "Come on." She grinned. "We've got hidden treasures to find."

Constance slept better than she had since before the day she was supposed to be married. At the time, she'd chalked the insomnia up to wedding jitters, but now she wasn't so sure. Could her subconscious have known all along that she and Marcus weren't right for each other?

Now that she'd put that behind her, at least in her mind, she had slept like a log. Or possibly she had worn herself out antiquing at Round Top. They came away with some amazing finds. She couldn't wait to get back to the shop and arrange them into displays and photograph them for *Antique Treasures*.

The suite was quiet. Beth and Annette left for the airport early that morning to get back to their jobs. As Constance's business partner, Beth could have stayed in Texas longer, but she was anxious to get back to the shop…and to Jeff.

Constance envied her that kind of relationship.

Dru was still asleep. At first, she had planned on leaving in the morning as well but had extended her stay to *keep an eye on Constance*, but last night Annette had called her out, tattling that

Dru wanted to spend extra time with a certain ginger cowboy.

Dru had actually blushed.

As long as they'd known each other, Constance couldn't recall ever seeing her friend flustered like that, especially over a guy. The guys were usually the ones hot under the collar.

Dance picked her up in that old military jeep of his and drove out to the other end of Chapel Pines. He pulled into the lot in front of a pleasant looking senior center and grinned. "Ready?" He leaned over and pulled an envelope out of the glove box.

"Uh-huh." Constance pulled the scrunchie from her hair and attempted to smooth it down after the ride over before she pulled it back up into a ponytail again.

Dance watched the process as though making a ponytail was as fascinating as a world-renowned artist painting.

"This is your grandfather we're seeing?" she asked as they walked across the small lot. Bright flowers in large pots cheered the entrance.

"Yes, my father's dad."

"He's a McCagan then."

"Yep, third generation born in America. His great grandfather came straight out to Texas and never left. Dug in his heels," Dance announced with a hitch of pride.

It really was pretty cool to have roots run deep in one place. The McCagans were all connected here, by land and a bold bloodline.

Exotic drumbeats hit them when Dance pulled open the door. "I forgot. It's Zumba hour."

"Zumba?"

Dance's grin widened. "They're still at the moving for exercise stage. I don't expect they'll go on tour anytime soon."

Cheeky guy. She bumped his arm with hers.

"Hey there, Dance," the lady at the front desk called out. "You bringing pretty young ladies around to call on your grandpa?" She smiled warmly at Constance.

"Oh, Dance, early visit this week?" Another lady in scrubs called out as she exited a room. "Your granddaddy's in the rec room. He's in rare form today." She chuckled as she went across the hall and into another room.

"I don't doubt it." Dance saluted with the envelope.

"He has got the moves today," the lady at the desk concurred.

Constance took the rapid exchange in. It was obvious Dance spent enough time here to know a few of the staff. Strike that. Apparently, he knew everybody here as they walked into the rec room and was greeted by staff and residents alike. One of the workers, going by his scrubs and the fact he was only in his thirties, was pounding out the beat on a Congo drum, while at least ten seniors were in the center of the room, moving in any way they could. Two of the ladies were on their feet, attempting to move hips back and forth in an imitation of the instructor, who not much younger than those she instructed, could move with a flexibility that any stripper would envy. She wore a bright pink leotard over flower patterned tights and danced with a joy that could get the sternest of drill sergeants to tapping their toes.

Several of the seniors sat in wheelchairs, moving their shoulders and shimmying with the beat the best they could. The ancient guy in the middle of it all, was wheeling his electric wheelchair back and forth with the controls at the end of the arm while he was whipping his other arm like a lasso around the beaten cowboy hat on his head, occasionally whooping out "yee-haw" in a wallop of glee.

It was the oddest, most delightful scene Constance had ever come upon. There couldn't be a happier group of seniors in all of Texas.

The seniors who weren't dancing, sat around the edges of the room, clapping, and enjoying the show. One of the ladies near the door, clasped Dance's hand and removed her oxygen mask so she could talk.

Her voice was soft and the drum too loud for Constance to hear what she said, but Dance leaned down, patting her hand as he held it. Whatever he said had the woman smiling and blushing beneath her parchment thin skin.

Pulling Constance over, he introduced her and before she knew it Dance was making the rounds to have a few words with each of the seniors who weren't busy spiraling their hips, bringing her along in tow. The women were friendly, eyeing her with speculation. No doubt wondering if she was someone special for Dance to be bringing around and her heart thumped as she realized she would like to be his someone special.

The gentlemen were charming, teasingly so as they called her a Yankee, asking how she was enjoying her visit to the south. Two of the men were telling her a story, something about a mule and the railway that she could barely make out over the music. She glanced at Dance who was crouched in front of another woman. He had set the envelope down on the floor so he could hold both of her frail hands while he listened intently to what she was saying.

Constance's heart took a little tumble.

Were there really guys like this in the world?

It wasn't an act. These people knew him and loved him. Their eyes lit and smiles grew when his attention focused on them.

He obviously came to visit his grandfather frequently and during those visits he'd spared time for the other residents as well.

She tried to transpose Marcus's image over Dance's, see him crouched and holding an old woman's hands, but she just couldn't see it.

The man talking to her said something outlandish.

"The mule did what?" She had been listening even as her gaze wandered to Dance. But what was that?

"Plum sat in the dirt and said he

wasn't moving," the gentleman said again with a devilish spark in his eyes.

"He didn't actually speak though," she corrected.

"He sure as tooting did." He grinned. "Sat there stubborn as rain and refused to budge. Had a mouth on him too. Cussed like a sailor denied leave."

"But—" Constance shook her head, trying to decide if there was any ounce of truth to any of the story or if the entire tale was fabricated.

"You gentlemen aren't trying to test my gullibility with embellishments, are you?"

"Now little darlin', we wouldn't do that." He feigned innocence.

"Besides, around here…" The other guy spread age-spotted hands over his paunchy belly. "We cut to the chase and call it bull. And this old coondog—" He flicked his thumb toward his friend. "—is piled hip-deep in it."

Constance laughed just as the drumbeat cut

off. These guys were adorable. She offered each her hand. "It was so nice to meet you."

"You're welcome to come anytime, duchess."

"I'd really like that." Maybe she could squeeze in another visit before she left next week.

"Jeb, Royse." Dance was back by her side. "You two behaving yourselves?"

"Like a boy scout," the storyteller's face puckered like a Shar Pei.

The other guy turned on him. "You weren't never a scout a day of your miserable life."

"I grew up on a ranch. Think I needed some fancy pancy organization to teach me what I grew up doing every durn day of my life? I'll give you a square knot." He raised his bony fist.

Dance drew Constance away from the entertaining quarrel to the gentleman who'd been rocking it in the electric wheelchair. "Constance, this is my grandfather, Lee McCagan."

"It's a pleasure to meet you, Mr. McCagan." Constance extended her hand.

He took it within both of his and winked at Dance. "She's a looker."

"Gramps, she's a friend. I told you to be on your best behavior."

"Oh gripes, at my age good behavior is overrated."

"And not near as much fun." The Zumba instructor breezed over, moved in front of Mr. McCagan, forcing Constance to step back, and planted a loud smacking kiss on his lips. "See you on Thursday." With the same fluidity of motion, she turned to Constance and grinned. "Don't worry none about his flirtations. He's harmless, honey. A tiger without bite."

"I've got plenty of bite left in me, Ruby," he called after her brightly colored retreating back.

"Sure you do," Dance agreed jovially.

"Besides," Mr. McCagan went on. "I've never met a woman who minds being told she's pretty." He smiled up at Constance beneath the brim of his hat.

"You called her a looker, not pretty," Dance said. His tone sounded stern, but his eyes were grinning. "And you said it to me, not her. There's a difference."

Lee's smile widened. "Did I offend you, sugar?"

Chuckling, she shook her head. "No, not at all."

He turned a smug I-told-you-so smile up at Dance.

"She's merely being polite," Dance informed. He shook his head. "Let's get you to your room. We have something to show you."

They started walking, but stopped to look at Lee who hadn't moved. "Are you coming?"

"Yeah, I'm waiting for you to go ahead so I can get a gander at those legs."

Constance laughed out loud even as Dance gawked back in horror. She couldn't help it. His grandfather had a streak of ornery as wide as a football field.

Not having it, Dance pointed toward the doorway, and unrepentant Lee McCagan thumbed his chair into motion.

"Wyatt stopped by earlier," Lee said as they moved through the wide corridor. "As soon as Ruby's class began, he hightailed it out of here like a rabbit in her crosshairs."

Dance chuckled. They entered Lee's room and the first thing Constance noticed were all the pictures on the walls, all framed, even the colorful crayon drawing of a stick family in front of an impossibly huge sun created by a child's hand. Brighton signed her name in bold green letters across the bottom, squeezing on a much smaller "n" when she ran out of room at the end. The other pictures were an assortment of family, some old black and whites, while others were recent and then everything in between. She moved closer to look at a picture taken of a much younger Dance in padded football gear, his dark hair longer and curling around his ears.

"Time to take your vitals, Lee." One of the staff walked in, pulling her stethoscope from around her neck, disrupting the thick ponytail of curly hair. "You staying in your chair or want to get in the bed?"

"Recliner for now, Crystal. I want to watch Days of Our Lives after my visit."

"You and your soaps." Crystal hummed. With Dance's assistance, Crystal had him out of the wheelchair and comfortably in his recliner in no time. They were an efficient team.

Crystal held Lee's wrist while she watched her watch before pressing her stethoscope to his chest.

"Think we're all going to have heart failure after every time we kick up our heels," Lee muttered. "How's Elise? In your opinion. Wyatt said she's backsliding."

The sudden lowering of Dance's shoulders was infinitesimal. "The doctors said we should keep an eye out for depression. It's common with people who've had strokes. I don't think she's there, but…" Dance pushed his hand back through his hair like a shrug. "She's not taking any interest in getting herself better."

Constance listened unobtrusively. She had no idea one of the McCagans had had a stroke. She wondered how bad it was and if there was anything she could help out with while she was here. They had all been so kind to her.

Lee waved the idea of depression off. "Bah, she's just stubborn. I know my daughter-in-law. When she decides she wants to help with her own recovery, she'll do it. But it has to be on her terms."

Dance nodded, unconvinced, a weariness Constance hadn't noticed before settled into the tiny lines between his dark brows. She fisted her hands by her sides, controlling the unbidden urge to smooth away the lines for him.

Dance sighed. "You know, Gramps, you can always come live at the inn where we can all look after you better."

"What? And leave my social life here? Place would fall to pieces without me."

"Think we can't get on without your old bag of

bones around here?" Crystal replaced her stethoscope around her neck.

"You know you would."

She laughed. "We'd miss you, Lee. I'll give you that."

He grinned.

"But right now, your O2 level is down," Crystal said. "I'm going to put you on oxygen for a bit." She reached over to the panel above the bed and cranked the oxygen level to where she wanted it before unlooping the tubing and adjusting the nasal cannula in place beneath Lee's nose.

"Is he all right?" Dance's brows furrowed.

"Nothing to worry about." Crystal watched the oximeter level. "It usually goes down a bit after Miss Ruby comes to call. "It will come back up after a while as long as he keeps that on." She patted Dance's arm on her way out the door and left them alone in the room.

"So, what's this visit about then?" Lee laced his long fingers across his middle. "Not that

I'm opposed to you bringing a pretty gal along with your ugly mug, but you haven't brought a woman along with you since that peroxided number. What was her name?"

"Sally Ann and you know darn well who she is. Martha and Bobby Jon's girl."

"Yeah, well, she was a piece of work. I didn't like seeing her getting her claws into you."

"She didn't get her claws…" Dance exhaled in exasperation. "She's married with a kid on the way already. Let it go."

Constance's ears perked up, enjoying the banter over Dance's past girlfriend. Sally Ann, huh?

Dance wouldn't look at her. "Anyway, you're right. This isn't a usual visit. Constance here is one of the guests at the inn. She's also an expert in antiques, and well, we found something in the carriage house that she's trying to help us learn more about."

It was the truth, however, being introduced as

a guest at the inn was kind of a let-down. Then again, how should he introduce her? That's all she really was to him. They weren't really even friends, hadn't known each other long enough to be.

"All right," Lee said. "What did you find?"

Dance looked to Constance to go on. "It's a bridal comb, made out of tortoiseshell." Lee looked at her as though he had no idea what she was describing. "We have a picture."

Dance took the picture out of the envelope and passed it to his grandfather. "We were hoping that you could tell us who this is."

Lee grabbed his glasses off the nightstand and put them on. "Ah, yes, that's…I forget her name."

Constance's pulse sped up. "But you recognize her?"

"Oh yes. I was very young at the time, seven or so, but I remember. This was my uncle's bride. Uncle Edward. He was my dad's youngest brother. My mother was in a tizzy because she wanted to do the wedding right even though she had very little time to put it together as many weddings were pushed up in those days due to the war." Fondness softened the wrinkles around his eyes. "I was put to task, sent off to run any errand she could think of until I learned to make myself scarce during those couple of days and hide out in the pasture behind the carriage house."

Pulling a chair near him, Constance sank down onto it, clasping her hands tightly together to control her nervous energy. She didn't want to interrupt Lee's flow of memories, but he had stopped, was staring at the photograph.

"What happened?" Dance nudged.

Lee's gaze snapped up. "War. That's what happened. The second world war. Uncle Eddie left immediately after the ceremony. We learned days later that he was killed in a transport accident. Never even made it past New York."

ELEVEN

CONSTANCE closed her eyes. Thorns gouged at her heart, painful little stabs with ice-cold bite. The life Eddie and Peg planned together was ripped away before it began. The bride had left, too inconsolable to stay near Edward's family without him. Marcus leaving Constance humiliated at the altar didn't stand in comparison to this kind of heartbreak. In truth, her heart hurt more for the woman who wrote the letter than it did for herself.

"There was a letter inside the box that we found the antique comb in. It was written to an Ady from a Peg," she told him. Her voice rasped with emotion.

Dance slid his hand onto her shoulder. "Do either of those names sound familiar to you?"

"Well, Ady is my mother. Agnes. She was a fairly starched woman, felt she had to hold up the standard for proper etiquette. Only those closest to her were allowed to call her Ady. And Peg, yes, that was her name." His gaze lowered back to the photograph he held. "Eddie and Peg. They made a dashing couple. It was all so tragic, even to a seven-year-old. More so, when Peg left us too. She had become family. She could have stayed. She didn't have to leave us like that."

"Do you know what became of her?" Dance asked softly.

Lee shook his head. "My parents looked for her. I remember something about a private detective, but she was gone. We never heard from her again."

Constance's mind was running ahead. If a private detective was hired to look into Peg's disappearance, there would have been papers, contracts, receipts...if they still existed. It was a long shot... She gasped, struck by an awful reality. "They never got Peg's letter. Your parents. If the box was lost somehow in the carriage house all this time, they never got her letter."

Outside the senior center, Dance glanced across the Jeep at Constance. Her head was down, hands clasped in her lap. "You okay?"

"Yeah." She didn't look up. "It's all so sad."

He had to admit, knowing what had happened to Eddie and Peg had affected him more than he'd believed it would.

"You don't suppose Shannon would have any of those private detective papers in her old boxes?"

"There were only old photo albums in there."

"I guess it's a dead end, then."

Dance let his surprise show in the raising of his brows.

"What?" Tiny crinkles set in the bridge of her pert little nose.

"Nothing. That's just the first time I've seen any lack of enthusiasm."

"I still have enthusiasm for it." She huffed and folded her arms. "A lot of enthusiasm."

Dance smothered the grin that wanted to surface. "Okay."

"Okay?"

"Yeah."

"All right then." Her lips puckered into an adorable pout that he wanted to kiss away. He curled his palms around the large steering wheel at the wayward thought. She was off-limits. Definitely off-limits. He turned the key in the ignition and the old Jeep rumbled to life.

His sidewise glance at Constance proved she was still mulling it over.

"That's it. I know just where to go." He pulled out of the senior retirement home's lot, heading east.

"Where?" She looked over at him and Dance swore a man could get lost in those big baby blues.

"Courthouse records. But first, something to eat. Apparently, you get grouchy when you're hungry."

That brought out the smile he was angling for.

"I am not grouchy." She smoothed a hand down her ponytail. "But something to eat sounds great about now. Should we head back to the inn?"

"I've got something else in mind."

Ten minutes later, they pulled up to one of the sorriest looking strip malls in Chapel Pines. Dance knew there was a gold mine of culture inside. All the authentic Mexican cafés in Texas seemed to be housed in unassuming strip malls and Café Consuela was no different. The real deal. Hand rolled tortillas, fresh made salsa, and Tampico. This was the place where native Mexicans came for a taste of home.

He ordered Constance the *pollo poblano* with cream sauce and got the spicy *grande burrito* for himself.

Constance's eyes widened with bliss at her first taste. She had such expressive features. He could sit back and watch her for hours and listen to the animated cadence of her voice. A guy could consider himself fortunate to spend an hour in her company.

She told him about her family, a hint of sadness overlaid the obvious admiration she held for her deceased father.

"I'm sorry." Reaching across the table, he covered her hand. "A girl ought to have a father around."

Her hand trembled beneath his. Their eyes met. Held. It was the most serious look she'd given him as though she searched his very soul. Warmth flushed through his veins, settling deeply into his chest.

"Thank you for that." She finally looked away and Dance felt the immediate loss of connection like a physical jolt. "I imagine you miss your father as well."

"Yeah." He squeezed her hand, not ready to relinquish it. "Yeah, I do. We lost him to a heart attack. He died between the space of one step to another one night after one of my football practices." He didn't know why he was telling her this. He never talked about that night with anyone, not even his family.

"You were there, then?"

"He came to pick me up. I was still too young to drive." His voice thickened. "I caught him when he fell, eased him to the ground, but he was already gone. I just didn't know it yet."

"I'm so sorry. That must have been so hard."

He nodded, the muscles in his throat tight.

"You must know what a gift that was, you being there with him, getting to watch you practice before…" she trailed off, her eyes misty.

He'd never thought of it like that, yet his dad had loved watching him on the field, had gone to every game. Football was one of the few times his usually quiet father had been demonstrative, even cracking the occasional grin.

His dad had been happy that night, relaxed, had squeezed Dance's shoulder in approval with a quick grin and then fallen while Dance screamed for help and started CPR, desperately hoping he was doing it right, until his coach ran over and gently pushed him aside to take over.

Constance was right. His father's last thoughts were of him. Good thoughts. Then he was gone.

Dance sat back in his chair, somehow feeling lighter than he had in a decade. "Let's skip the courthouse for now. I want to show you something."

"Oh, okay." Her brow crinkled in puzzlement, yet ever inquisitive and impulsive, Constance was ready to go with whatever he had in mind. Rather than ask where they were going, she set back to guessing his name. The woman was relentless.

"Frankincense?"

"What kind of name is that?" Dance scowled from his side of the Jeep.

"A biblical one." One dainty little shoulder lifted in a shrug. "I heard it in a movie once."

"What kind of movie has a name like that?"

"An old classic." Constance grinned. "Are you saying that Frankincense is a more terrible name than whatever yours is?"

"I didn't say anything." Dance clamped his mouth shut. As far as he was concerned, his real name and Frankincense were on about the same level.

"Cecil then. You look like a—ohhhh." Constance stood in the footwell to see over the windshield as he slowed to a stop. They'd gone up a slight hill and the field in front of them was awash in vibrant blues.

"Is this what you wanted to show me?" She smiled down at him. "It's beautiful." She hopped out of the Jeep and ran over to the old wooden fence. "Can we go in?"

"Sure, but step lightly. Merle will have my hide if we crush the blossoms."

"Does this Merle own the field?"

"You'd think he does by the way he patrols it."

"I've seen postcards of Texas bluebonnets, but photographs don't do it justice."

Dance leaned back against the Jeep as enamored with the woman as she was with the field before her. She made a fine picture with her slender back to him and hands on the top rail of the old cattle fence and the ends of her sunny ponytail lifting in the warm breeze.

He had to capture this moment. Taking his phone from his pocket, he snapped a shot.

Hearing the slight click, Constance looked over her shoulder. "Did you just take a picture?"

"Made too pretty of one not to," he answered honestly.

Her reaction shouldn't have surprised him as she pulled out her own cell. "Let's take one of us together. Oh dang, my battery's dead. You'll have to send them to me. C'mere."

Always read to oblige a pretty gal, Dance

strode over to the fence and held out the phone. "Say cheese."

"Cheese." Constance tucked in next to him—she smelled so good—and they mugged a quick succession of shots for the camera.

"Let's see." She plucked the phone from his grasp. "Ha, your eyes are closed in this one. I, however, look awesome."

"If you say so yourself," he teased and leaned in close to have his own look at them. She did look great. In fact, apparently, the woman couldn't take a bad picture, while he was caught in all sorts of awkward half grins. Most photos captured him with straight lips. His sisters called it his angry camera face. Which he really didn't care one way or another about, except…he looked closer, the brim of his hat brushing Constance's. He looked happy.

In every shot.

Awkward, but happy.

"Oh my gosh, look at this one." Constance bubbled with laughter over a shot where both of their cheesy smiles were so wide their eyes were mere slits.

He revised his earlier assumption. She could take a bad picture. Laughter rose up through his chest.

"I'm sending these to my phone." She sighed on a laugh and started putting her number into his cell without a hint of inhibition in giving out her number and Dance tried not to read anything into it.

"Okay, sent them." Constance looked up, her smile bright before it slipped into an indefinable expression as she must have noticed Dance was no longer smiling along with her.

His thoughts had scattered as his senses took control.

They were so close, her upturned face inches from his. Her lips parted slightly, and her eyes widened.

As though his hands moved of their own volition, he tucked a wisp of her hair behind her ear.

The next thing he knew his lips were on hers, his arm had moved to the swell of her hip and he was pulling her close. Everything after that was pure instinct.

She was soft breezes and satin, as intoxicating as the finest Charbonneau and as sweet as dew on a sunny morning.

She pressed into him, kissing him back with the same passion she threw into everything she did.

Marcus Wentworth was a grade-A idiot to walk away from her.

Dance internally flinched. He pulled back. Constance's eyes were bright, her skin flushed, lips swollen from his kiss, and she was the darnedest most beautiful thing he'd ever set eyes on. And…he couldn't do this. He wanted to. Storms almighty he wanted to. He wanted to kiss her until the chickens went to roost, but she was engaged for Pete's sake. Or had been up until a few days ago.

His heart hurt like a cold hand reached in and twisted the burning organ like taffy. Constance was hurting, in love with a guy who wasn't worthy of her, and Dance couldn't be the guy to step in and take advantage when she was at her most vulnerable.

He dropped his hands to his sides, took a full step back.

Hurt immediately swamped her expression. She folded her arms around herself, looking small and forlorn. It took every last resolve Dance had not to take her back into his arms.

She felt right in his arms. He shoved his hands into his pockets.

Her eyes shimmered. "I'm sorry. I don't know what that was." This time she took a step away.

"No, I'm sorry. I shouldn't have…" He slammed a hand back through his hair. "It's my fault. I shouldn't have taken advantage."

Her head jerked up at that. "Advantage? Please, I'm an adult. We both got caught up in a moment. Let's leave it at that. Just..." She shrugged, brushing it off. "Let's forget it ever happened."

"Sure." Dance rocked back on his boot heels. He couldn't speak for her, but he wouldn't be forgetting that kiss short of a sledgehammer dislodging it from his brain.

Numbly, he followed her back to the WILLYS, climbed in and turned the ignition.

"Do you mind if we go to the courthouse tomorrow?" Constance looked out the windshield, avoiding his gaze.

"Sure," he answered dumbly, everything he wanted to say, or for that matter how to phrase it, was stuck in his chest.

She glanced at him, then quickly away. "It's just that I haven't spent much time with Dru. It doesn't have anything to do with…" Her fingers waggled in the air between them. Her shoulders lifted and fell with a sigh. "Okay, we both know that's not true."

His hand twitched on the wheel. He was

ultra-aware of her beside him, of every movement she made, the varying tones of her voice.

She began playing with the ends of her ponytail, her gaze set on the road ahead. "We kissed. It happened. It was nice. Really nice actually, but neither of us are ready to go there." The quick glance she took at his profile shouldn't have had the power to rev up his pulse like it did. He missed a pothole and the Jeep bounced, jostling them forward.

Constance steadied herself with a hand on the windshield bar. She took a long inhalation. "Anyway, we're both feeling a little awkward now, so I think it's best we call it a day and get back to it tomorrow—the courthouse records, I mean."

He didn't know it was possible to feel someone blush, but there it was, he felt it even though his eyes remained stoically front and center.

"Okay," he agreed.

He felt her gaze turn to him, this time a few seconds longer before she turned away.

She picked at a non-existent thread on her slacks. "I just think the awkwardness will run out if we give it a day and we'll be back on even ground tomorrow."

"Agreed."

She threw her hands up. "Can you please give me something other than one-word replies?"

"Okay."

She turned sideways in the passenger seat and gave him a look bland enough to bleach sand.

"Sorry."

TWELVE

"WHAT'S wrong?" Dru pounced on her the moment Constance stepped into the suite.

"Nothing." Constance sank down onto the pretty flower-patterned sofa.

"There's definitely something wrong." Dru put her earring in. She looked nice in a halter top sundress, a little less flamboyant than her usual style, but it was obvious she was on her way out. "Spill."

"He kissed me."

Dru's head jerked up in mid-process of slipping on her strappy wedges. "The handsome inn owner?"

Constance nodded.

Dru beamed. "Well, that's what you wanted, isn't it? A good-looking guy to take your mind off Marcus for a while. How's it working?"

Completely. "Marcus who?" she murmured.

Dru lowered beside her, one shoe dangling in her hand. "It's not what you wanted?"

"I wanted a little distracting flirting, yes, but…"

"You like him." Dru sighed.

"More than I have a right to." Constance sloughed back, crushing her head against the plush sofa back. "What's wrong with me? I was all set to spend the rest of my life with Marcus, but now I think I dodged what could have been the biggest mistake of my life. And I have all these tangled up feelings for Dance. I really like him, but that's just trying to fill up the hole left by Marcus, right?"

"You just said marrying him would have been a mistake." Dru's brows rose.

"It would have, but that doesn't mean I no longer care for him." Constance huffed out a breath.

"And you're afraid you're using Mr. Yummy to fill in the holes?" Dru pursed her lips, looking every bit the detective figuring out the inner workings of Constance's mind.

"Exactly." Constance threw up her hands. "He doesn't deserve that."

"Oh, honey, you're overthinking this." Dru tapped Constance's knee. "Believe me, when it comes down to it, there's not many guys who wouldn't mind being used for a few days. It's harmless."

Constance pulled one of the sofa pillows onto her lap to absently run her fingers along the tassels. "Dance is different."

A knock sounded at the door.

"That's Austin." Dru grinned almost nervously. "His mom is having a barbeque." Her eyes took on a shine Constance had never seen before. "He wants me to meet his parents." She ducked her head.

Constance scooted up straighter. "But you don't do parents."

"I know." Dru took the pillow from her and buried her face in it.

The knock sounded again.

Constance nudged her. "Better not keep him waiting."

Dru lowered the pillow. "I could cancel, stay here with you while you're down in the dumps."

"Nice try." Constance took the pillow back. "Go meet the future in-laws."

Dru froze halfway up to standing. "In-laws?" Her cheeks reddened across skin that suddenly went pale.

"I'm kidding." Alarmed, Constance backtracked. A panicking Dru was never a good thing. "You're just having a little fun with Austin. Nothing more."

"Right." Dru breathed deeply, smoothing out her skirt. "A little fun."

Constance refrained from mentioning the

cowboy had Dru all in knots and acting completely different than she had with any other of her beaus. She didn't want to scare her off.

Dru still hadn't moved to answer the door. "Maybe I should stay."

"Nonsense, go have a good time."

"Or you could come with…?"

Constance shook her head, too out of sorts to navigate through a family barbeque. "You're sweet, but I'm going to soak in the tub and overthink my life."

The bath didn't clear her thoughts like she'd hoped, though she lingered until the water cooled and she was hungry. She thought about ordering room service and try to quiet her thoughts curled up on the big bed with a movie, but decided she'd rather get out of the room for a bit.

She'd make a quick run downstairs, grab

some dinner, and if she happened to see Dance then she might be able to tell if butterflies still skimmed around her insides at the sight of him.

Maybe that was just a one-time thing from an unexpected kiss. It'd taken her off guard. And yeah, he was attractive. She'd feel as off centered by any guy kissing her so soon after Marcus. Wouldn't she?

No. Her heart whispered no.

She ordered cheese and broccoli soup, eating it at the bar so she had a full view of the lobby beyond. Dance never walked past, and Constance was more disappointed by that than she wanted to admit. That should tell her something about her own feelings.

What a mess.

Frustrated with herself, she wandered around the inn, checking out the exercise room and the laundry facilities, until she ended up in a pretty sunroom at the back side of one of the wings.

She walked among the plants and flowers, not

realizing anyone was there until she came upon the sitting area and a woman quietly watching her from a rocker.

"Oh, I'm sorry. I didn't mean to intrude."

"Oh...it's...okay." The woman had a difficult time speaking. Constance looked closer, noticing how one side of her face drooped lower than the other. Even so, she had an uncanny resemblance to...

"Are you Dance and Shannon's mother?"

He found her in the sunroom with his mother. The sight before him rooted him to the spot just inside the entrance.

His mom was fully engaged, leaning slightly forward in her chair.

With the fluttery gestures and nods he'd come to recognize when she was excited about something, Constance had his mom's full attention.

Yet…there was more going on.

Constance was perched on the edge of the coffee table, leaning in close to his mom. They reminded him of conspiring teenagers with their heads close together. Constance waited as though she expected his mother to answer. He sighed, she didn't understand how difficult it was for his mom to form sentences or how embarrassed she got when she tried. Especially in front of strangers.

He readied to come to both their rescues when he saw it.

His throat tightened. They were communicating in a way none of them had been able to since the stroke.

Elise took Constance's hands in her own and spoke a complete sentence. "No difference at all. My husband, when I first…" Once more frustration overtook her features.

"Was it love at first sight?" Constance asked in

a whisper frosted with awe.

His mom shook her head and smiled. There was a twinkle in her eyes. "Not at...at first. Took—"

Constance waited patiently.

"At...at least th—three dates before..." Elise looked at Constance with hope and what was transpiring sunk into Dance's awareness like a smack to the back of his head. He got it. They'd all been babying her, expecting their mom to be the same as she had before. But Constance never knew her like that. She had no expectations and was communicating with her without boundaries.

"Then it hit you," Constance said. "An overwhelming punch to the heart that you can't make sense of?"

His mom nodded. "Exactly that."

Throat tight, Dance backed out of the room before either woman noticed he had been there at all.

THIRTEEN

CONSTANCE enjoyed her talk with Dance's mom. She was an amazing woman and had settled some things in her mind.

Smiling, she left the sunroom and headed toward the elevator to go up to her room.

"Constance?"

Everything inside of her stilled at his voice. Her breath caught in her throat. She couldn't turn around. Her pulse banged loudly in her ears.

"Constance," he said again.

Slowly, she turned. He stood there, immaculate in his dark suit, not one hair out of place. "Marcus, what are you doing here?"

Would it have killed him to look disheveled

like he'd been torn up about leaving her?

"I made a mistake." He rubbed his palm down his thigh. "I got cold feet at the last moment. I don't know. But I've had time to think things through, and…everything's wrong without you."

It was exactly what she wanted to hear, yet then again, it wasn't. The elevator dinged open. She stood very still, trying to find an ounce of feeling. As much as it was satisfying to hear him say he wanted her back and that it was a mistake, it wasn't. She wasn't relieved. She wasn't happy to see him at all.

"You humiliated me on what should have been the happiest day of our lives together." Okay, so she had to rub salt in the wound a little. She was entitled, but even her voice didn't betray any strong feeling behind it.

Marcus didn't notice. "I know." He closed the distance between them and took her hands in his. They felt soft. "I'll spend the rest of my life making that up to you, baby. I'm so very regretful."

She felt the gaze of the blond woman at the check-in counter on them. Quietly, the woman lifted the phone to her ear, determination edged in her jaw. Her body seemed rigid, coiled, like she was ready to jump in. That was the last thing Constance needed.

"Regretful," she echoed Marcus, trying the word out on her tongue. "No." She shook her head.

"No?" Bewilderment lifted his eyes. He clearly hadn't expected that.

"No," Constance spoke softly, feeling the growing conviction take root in her chest. "Yes, no." She stood and moved away if only to get her hands out of his. She walked toward the large entrance doors. Several other people had stopped what they were doing, pretending not to be listening when her gaze floated over them. She turned back to Marcus. "You were right to do what you did. Of course it would have been nice to have a little warning, cancel the flowers and catering. Do you know how much money went into that?"

Marcus stood. "You are angry. I deserve that. Baby, I'll make it all up to you. I promise. We'll set a new date." He advanced toward her, arm out to take her hand again.

"No." She side-stepped away. "That's the thing. I'm not mad. Not at what I should be anyway. Don't you think that's strange? I should be furious. Upset. Crying my eyes out that I lost you, but…I don't feel any of that." She looked up at his incredulous features, hoping to make him understand.

The woman at the check-out was on the phone, talking quietly into the receiver.

Constance spoke a little quieter. "I don't think I loved you as much as I thought I did. I was in love with the idea of you. I was in love with being married to a dashing intelligent man." She reached up and smoothed his hair off of his forehead. "And you are all that, but…" She shook her head. "I don't think we were really in *love* love, the kind of passion where you can't wait to see the other person or hear their voice on the phone. We were just kind of playing our parts."

She paced away from him. "They were good parts to play, but when the curtain came down and the stage lights went off, what would we have then?"

"Constance, honey, you don't mean that. You're angry and trying to punish me."

"No, I'm not. Listen to what I'm telling you. We are not getting back together. I am not going to be your wife."

"Of course we are."

"You felt something was off. Otherwise, you wouldn't have walked away."

"I told you it was cold feet. I was an idiot, is that what you want to hear?"

"Actually yes, but that doesn't change the fact that you saved us both from the biggest mistake of our lives."

"And I was wrong." He tried to take her hand again, but she shrugged him off. He sighed.

"I'm trying to make it up to you, but you're being stubborn and won't let it go."

She wasn't getting anywhere. They were just going around and around. "I don't want to hurt you, Marcus, but I don't want to be with you anymore. I'm sorry."

"You're my fiancé. You'll get over this in a few days. Let's pack your bags and come home with me. You'll feel better when you're home."

Constance buried her face in her hands. Once Marcus made up his mind, he had blinders on that let him see only his goal. It made him great at his job, but she wasn't liking that quality too much right now. What *she* wanted wasn't even in his peripheral. She doubted he heard anything she said.

She lowered her arms. "Marcus, go home. Take some time to think about this, really think about it."

He frowned down at her. "I did, and the conclusion that I came to was that I'm better with you."

"You're better. What about me?"

"What?"

"What about me? Am I better with you?"

"Of course you are."

"How would you know? Were we happy Marcus? You and I?"

"What are you talking about? Of course we were. We were content. We worked well together."

"Worked well together. Is that what marriage is?"

"It's not all fun and games all the time." His nostrils flared. "Is that what you expect?"

"No, but I do expect someone who isn't going to run away when he gets uncomfortable, and I would expect to care more about it when he did. Marcus, are you listening? When you left me, I wasn't sad. I was relieved."

Nobody moved. The people around them gawked, not even trying to pretend they weren't eavesdropping.

Marcus's eyes went wide in disbelief. Constance was trembling. That was harsh. She shouldn't have been so harsh.

"I see." Marcus shuttered his expression behind a blank façade.

She sighed. "Marcus, I'm not trying to hurt you. I just…do I fill the parts of you that are empty? Those parts that you didn't realize needed to be filled?"

He stared at her. "You're not making any sense."

"I'm making perfect sense. At least if we loved each other, it would make sense. I don't want to be just a couple that works well together, who is content. I want passion, and laughter. I want you to argue with me when you think I'm wrong and feel empty when I'm not with you. I wanted you to love me."

"I do love you."

She shook her head. "No, no you don't. You think you do, but you don't."

He stared at the floor.

The doors flew open, and Mr. Larie strode in, rifle in hand. "He the one?" He swung the barrel up, receiving end inches from Marcus's nose.

Alarmed, Constance grabbed onto Mr. Larie's arm. "You're not going to shoot him."

"Someone needs to."

"Constance?" Marcus squeaked.

"He's not going to shoot you." She glared at Mr. Larie. "Are you?"

"Thinking about it. He bothering you?"

"No, he was just leaving."

"No, I'm not," Marcus argued.

Mr. Larie adjusted his grip on his rifle, causing it to slide forward.

Marcus leaned his head back yet held his ground. "Not without Constance."

"Yes, without Constance," she practically growled. "We're done, Marcus. It's over. There's no going back."

"You don't mean—"

"I do mean it. I've never been so sure of anything in my life. I don't want to marry you."

"Only because—"

"Do you really need me to say it?"

Marcus frowned. He looked at her, really seemed to look.

She held his gaze, letting him look his fill, hoping he would see her resolve and finally get it. At long last, he nodded. Looking at Mr. Larie, he nudged the rifle barrel away, straightened his jacket, and walked out the door.

Dance braked hard in the circle driveway of the inn, sending the Jeep skidding sideways as it came to an abrupt stop. He'd made a full U-turn on the roadway when Chalese called him from the front desk. He wasn't even sure what he was going to do about it, just that he needed to be there.

He shot out of the Jeep and ran up the steps right as a man in a tailored suit ran out of the inn and shoved past him. "Watch it," the guy barked.

On his heels, Clete stepped out, but remained on the porch, his old rifle cradled along his arm.

"This isn't finished," the guy called back at Clete.

In answer, Clete simply cocked the rifle.

Dance swiveled his head back around fast enough to cause whiplash. "Is that him?" Unspent energy buzzed through him like lightning on a stormy night. His hands curled into fists. He took a step down.

"Let it go, son." Clete's voice rode low in the saddle. "I've run the fella off."

The fella glared back at them, before barking at TJ, their youngest valet. "Get my car!"

Bristling, Dance ran down the stairs, and jerked the man—Constance's runaway groom—around by his arm. "Hey, you don't treat our staff like that."

Marcus jerked his arm free. "Who are you?"

Car doors slammed. Dance caught a bare glimpse through his narrowed angry haze of Wyatt and Austin coming out of Austin's truck.

"I'm the owner of The McCagan." Dance widened his stance like a junkyard dog guarding his territory. "Do we have a problem…Sir?" he ground out.

Marcus visibly got himself back under control. It was a remarkable transformation, like putting on a mask. His features smoothed. He straightened his tie.

"No, no problem." He gave a self-depreciating smile. "Just a little personal business that went awry. My apologies. I haven't been my best of late." He reached into his jacket and pulled out his billfold. "As you say, there's no need to take it out on the staff." He handed TJ a fifty-dollar bill. "Accept this as an apology for my rude behavior."

TJ's eyes went wide. He looked at Dance for an indication of what to do.

"Get the gentleman his car." The hostile edge rasped through Dance's voice.

"Thank you, sir. It wasn't no big deal." Jimmy ran off to retrieve Marcus's car. The sooner the man was off their property the better. Dance remained planted on the step; arms folded.

Marcus glanced up at him. His Adam's apple bounced. Good. "You have a lovely inn." Guess he thought the moment required small talk.

Dance nodded. "We like it." He spotted Levi coming around from the back. Small town gossip mill had worked fast. All his friends were narrowing in to have his back. Not that he needed them to handle a little pris in his fancy suit and calm demeanor.

One who obviously was uncomfortable in long silences. Marcus rocked on his feet. "My fiancé and I had planned on coming here for our honeymoon."

"You don't say." Dance asked just for spite. "What happened?"

Marcus waved his hand like he was

shooing flies. "Oh, you know, misunderstanding, that sort of thing. I came all this way to make things right and find my lovely bride is being stubborn."

"Hmmm," Dance hummed noncommittally, his temper a rancid burn low in his belly. Where was the dang car?"

A sleek BMW rental finally pulled into the driveway. Relief unclamped Dance's rigid spine a centimeter. "I'm sorry things didn't work out for you."

Marcus glanced up in surprise. "Oh no, it's just a little hiccup in our relationship. She's just pouting. It's nothing I won't be able to handle once my wayward fiancé is back home." He glanced up at Clete. "And can be reasoned with."

That did it. "You sonofa…" Dance swung, would have connected if Wyatt wasn't suddenly there, shoving him back up a step so forcefully he fell on his butt on the next step up.

"What is wrong with you people?" Marcus

shouted; his eyes blown wide.

"What's wrong with us?" Austin got into his face, forcing Marcus to back into the open door of his car that Jimmy had just come out of. "What's wrong with us is that we have a little common decency when it comes to our womenfolk. You make a commitment, you keep it. Leastwise, you don't run off on the day of the nuptials and leave your bride hanging without a word. That's plain cowardly."

Marcus's face reddened. He looked around at everyone watching him.

"Yeah, we all know," Austin poked a finger at his chest. "I suggest you git."

"It wasn't like…" Marcus stammered.

"We don't care," Wyatt said, and waggled his fingers. "Leave."

Jaw clenched, Marcus got into his car, slammed the door, and pulled out with squealing tires.

Levi lowered to sit on the step beside

Dance and Wyatt. "Well that made for an entertaining afternoon."

Dance was still hot under the collar. "I didn't need you to run interference."

"Nope," Wyatt agreed. "But the inn did. Can't imagine Mr. Fancypants wouldn't have sued for damages on his pretty face."

Dance deflated. "Point taken. But it sure would have been satisfying. Thanks, guys."

"Our pleasure." Austin grinned. "We haven't seen you this riled up since Frank Gamil tripped Betty Lou in the cafeteria."

"Yeah, well." Dance started to get up. "I need to go see Constance."

Both Wyatt and Levi pushed him back down by the shoulders. "Oh no you don't," Wyatt said. "After a confrontation with her ex, the last thing you want to do is show up. Trust me, bro. You do not want her feeling all guilty by leaning on your shoulder."

"That's ridiculous." Was it?

"If you really like her, you do not want to be the

rebound guy," Austin agreed.

"She's got to be hurting—"

"Dru's with her," Austin supplied. "I just texted and canceled our afternoon so she could stay with your gal."

His gal. Dance ached to be with her right now. "I don't know."

Mr. Larie spoke right behind them. "Listen to your pals, Dance. The last thing that little gal needs right now is to see you. She needs time. Give her that."

He'd give her anything. If time was what she needed, he'd give her time.

Before he could even form an answer, Wyatt hauled him to his feet. "I say we head to Sooty's and grab a beer."

Austin looked up at the entrance doors longingly. "Well, my afternoon suddenly freed up. You in, Levi?"

Levi glanced back the way he'd come from the carriage house. "I'm still working—"

Wyatt cut him off. "Boss says you can take a few hours."

Levi rolled his eyes. "Guess I'm good. Mr. Larie, you in?"

Clete tilted his head. "Now that I think about it, I'm a mite parched. Reckon I can tolerate that swill Sooty serves for a night."

"That's the spirit." Austin clapped the old vintner on the back and started walking toward his truck. "Did you hear that fella squeal when he thought Dance was going to deck him?" He started laughing.

"Thought for a moment one of Bek's pigs got loose. Made the same sound." Levi chuckled and soon they were all laughing and cramming into Austin's and Dance's respective vehicles.

FOURTEEN

THE confrontation with Marcus rattled her. Constance thought she loved him, but seeing him…there wasn't anything there, never had been besides the excitement of romance and steadiness of his presence. Turned out he wasn't that steady at all.

She lifted her suitcase onto the bed. She couldn't stay here any longer, mooning over Dance. If she really wanted to know how she felt about him, if her feelings for him were any more concrete than what she'd felt for Marcus, she had to put distance between them.

She paused, her hand on the hanger holding

Dru's blue sundress she'd worn when they went to Shannon's. The material wrinkled beneath her tightening hand.

It wasn't Marcus that was the problem. Or Dance. It was her. She no longer trusted herself, trusted her feelings. How could she? She had been going to marry someone she thought she loved, but turns out, she didn't.

She sank to the edge of the bed. "What am I going to do?"

She'd never be able to trust herself again after missing all the clues that she hadn't been in love with Marcus at all. How would she ever know when she was in love?

"Are we going somewhere?" Dru stood in the doorframe between the bedroom and the rest of the suite. "The honeymoon still has another week."

"The honeymoon never started." Tears wet Constance's lashes.

"Oh dollface." Dru sat beside her, slinging an arm over her trembling shoulders. "It can't be that bad that you have to leave early."

"Marcus showed up."

Dru stiffened. "I know. Austin told me."

Great. Everyone in Chapel Pines must know all about it. "He wants me back."

"Of course he does. You're the only thing that rumples his immaculate life."

Constance winced.

Dru squeezed her shoulder. "You know what I mean. You breathed life into his stuffy existence."

"Is that supposed to make me feel better?"

"Not at all. You have the right to be miserable. Want to break something?"

"No." Constance frowned. "Maybe. No. Everything in here belongs to the inn."

"Yeah, but Marcus is paying for the room. It will make you feel better." Dru grinned.

"Tempting, but no. The McCagans don't deserve that."

"Fine, we'll buy some china plates later." Dru's eyes lit up. "I bet Austin will let us shoot them with his rifle."

Constance laughed. "That actually sounds nice."

Constance set her bags by the check-in desk and knocked on the office door.

"Come in," Shannon sang out. She looked up from the desk as Constance entered. "Oh hey." Her sunny greeting faltered as her gaze took Constance in. "Is everything okay?" She got up and came around the desk.

Shaking her head, Constance closed the door. "I just wanted to say goodbye and thank you for all you've done."

"You're leaving? But you have the suite for several more days." Shannon squinted. "Did something happen?"

The misery bubbled out. "No. Yes. I don't know.

My fiancé—ex-fiancé was just here."

"He was?"

Constance nodded. "You've got to be the only one in town who doesn't know. He still wants to marry me."

Shannon stepped back. Lines appeared in her forehead. "Is that what you want?"

"No. Gosh no. It's over between us."

"Then why are you leaving?"

"I have to. I can't stay here, not with…"

"Not with my brother here," Shannon answered for her. "Do you care about him?"

Constance's eyes blurred with tears. "I do care for him. But I thought I loved Marcus. I can't just jump into a relationship. It's not fair to Dance. Oh, Shannon, I don't want to hurt him."

Shannon nodded. "I think you're right. You need to leave until you're sure about what you feel. Staying will only make that worse. Are you going to say goodbye to him?"

"I think he already said it."

"You spoke with him?"

"Not exactly." Constance blushed. "Last time we were together, he kissed me."

Shannon's eyes widened.

Constance hurried on before Shannon could say anything. "And then he backed off, said it was a mistake."

"Oh. What do you think?"

"I think it was wonderful, but scary. I don't want to hurt him, Shannon. I care about him too much to do that."

Shannon draped her arm around her shoulders. "Thank you for that. I don't want Dance hurt either."

"Will you tell him goodbye for me? I'd do it, I should do it, but…" Her shoulders sagged. "I'm afraid I'd just complicate things, make a mess of it, draw out more feelings that neither of us can be sure of. Or maybe I'm just chicken. Tell him I'll call him in a few days when my stomach isn't all in knots and I can think straight." Marcus's visit had really knocked her for a loop.

Shannon nodded. "I get it. I'll let him know, but Constance, once you figure it out, there will always be a room open here for you."

FIFTEEN

SHE'D only been home for two days when her mom summoned her over to her house. "I'll call Marcus, ask him to come over."

"Mom, you're not hearing me." Constance rubbed the pads of her fingers against her temples. "We're not reconciling. I don't love him. I don't want to marry him."

Her mom stopped pacing, phone in hand. "You don't know what you want. You're hurt right now, embarrassed."

"Embarrassed, yes, but I'll get over that. Hurt, not so much. Mom, please stop."

Her mom slid onto the sofa beside her. "All right. I'm listening. What do we need to do to get him back? You think letting him stew longer will work?"

Constance laughed. "Mom!"

"Marcus has been calling me, you know. He still loves you."

"He just thinks that he does. Up." Constance stood, waiting for her mom to follow suit. Instead, she just blinked up at her.

Shaking her head, Constance went into the kitchen. By the time she had the large mixing bowl on the counter and the eggs and milk out of the fridge, her mom had followed her in.

"What are you doing?"

"Making cookies."

"Now?"

"Yes. Will you get the baking soda and flour?"

Her mom went to the fridge. "I'm sure I have chocolate chips in here."

That brought Constance up short. "Really?"

Her mom gave her a quizzical look. "I've been known to make cookies on occasion." She broke the eggs into the bowl and started whisking.

Constance watched her, really looking at her. "I know," she said quietly. The achiness that had been part of her heart lightened. She wrapped her arms around her mom, leaning her head against her mom's temple. "I know you're only looking out for me."

Her mom went very still. She stopped beating the eggs. "Honey." She patted Constance's elbow. "You're my child."

"I know." Constance squeezed her mom's shoulders and let go. "Just...thank you for that. I love you, Mom."

Her mom pulled back to study her features. "Constance, are you okay?"

Warmth pulled at Constance's heart. "Yeah, Mom." She measured out the flour. "I really want to tell you about what happened in Texas."

It had been Grandma McCagan's tradition. Get the entire family together for dinner every second Sunday of the month, rain or shine. Grandma was no longer with them, but the tradition carried on.

Wyatt picked Gramps up from the senior retirement center while Chloe swung over to the inn to collect their mom. Even Cash arranged to video conference on the computer for a few minutes.

"Tell me about this Constance," Cash said the moment Dance sat in front of the laptop in Shannon's home office. Chloe had just vacated the chair and had obviously given her twin an earful.

Dance inwardly groaned. "She was a guest at the inn. She found an old bridal comb in the carriage house that belonged to our great grandmother and was helping us authenticate it. She's gone back home to Connecticut now."

"Uh-huh," Cash deadpanned. "That's not how Chloe and Shannon tell it. She got under your skin."

"Geez, Cash, why don't you come home, and we'll have a slumber party and gossip. Maybe braid each other's hair…"

"Wiseass." Cash leaned closer to his side of the screen as though they weren't across the ocean. "Touchy too. So why'd you run her off?"

"Because he's a moron." Wyatt came into the room and leaned in so Cash could see him. "Hey, kid, how's the desert treating you?"

"Hot. Dry. Same as last month. So why is this Constance all our sisters could talk about and how did big brother muck it all up?"

"I didn't muck up anything." Dance threw up his hands.

"She left a week early," Cash pointed out. Dance was going to throttle Chloe. "What'd you do to mess it up?"

He kissed her, got too close when she was already heartbroken. Let his heart get tangled up in her. "I didn't do anything."

"Maybe that's the problem." Wyatt

plunked onto the plush paisley patterned chair in the corner of Shannon's office.

Dance scowled. "She'd just been left at the altar. What kind of guy would I be if I took advantage of that?"

Cash pulled back; dark brows furrowed. "How long ago?"

"They booked the suite for their honeymoon," Wyatt informed.

"Ouch." Cash's face fell. "That's soon. I see the problem."

"Yeah." Dance's tone sounded as flat and empty of life as he felt.

For once Wyatt didn't have anything to say about it either.

"It's too bad," Cash ventured across the computer screen. "Because, dude, you look like a hound dog that lost his bone to the river. I'm sorry, man."

Dance shifted in his seat, uncomfortable with his family, even his brothers scrutinizing his feelings over Constance, when Cash brought up an even more uncomfortable topic. "How's mom?"

"All right, that's it." Shannon came right up to the check-in desk where Dance was filling in for Josh while he took his break. "I can't take it anymore."

"What?" Dance crinkled his brows, wondering what had Shannon in a tither.

"This." She waved her hand up and down in front of Dance's chest. "You. Mopey. You haven't cracked a smile in weeks."

"I don't mope." Dance pulled up the morning receipts to go over them.

"Oh, you mope all right." Shannon frowned. "We all see it. Get out your phone and call her."

"And say what?" Something strange kicked low in his stomach like a blunted strike with a baseball bat. "We weren't that close. I barely knew her a few days."

"I'm calling bull hockey on that one." Shannon covered her hands over his. "When you meet the right one, you know it, whether it's a few days or a few years. Besides, Dru tells me Constance is just as mopey as you are."

Dance flicked up his gaze. "You've been talking to Dru?"

"I saw her at Heather's bakery just an hour ago. You knew she moved in with Austin?"

"She did?" Surprise hit Dance square in the solar plexus.

"You were at Sooty's yesterday with him. Don't you guys talk?"

"We're guys. And there was a game on." That should be obvious. They weren't a bunch of women sharing and caring. He almost felt offended. "So Dru stayed?" He tried to ask casually as though it made no nevermind to him.

Shannon didn't buy it. "She's been back and

forth as though she can't make up her mind. Right now, she's here." Shannon dragged out the pause. "So, you want to know how Constance is pining away for you or not?"

Dance's heart stuttered like the WILLYS engine on a cold start before it purred to life. He was eager to hear any word of Constance. He'd nearly called her several times before coming to his senses and shoving his phone away. He'd searched the courthouse records for anything the private detective his grandparents had hired to find Peg might have left, just to have an excuse to call her. But there was nothing, a dead end.

The truth was, he missed her. She was on his mind twenty-four seven. His heart had gotten tangled up in her so quickly he didn't know how to unravel it. Time, he told himself, give it time and let the feelings fade. Or at least, give her the time to get over Marcus Wentworth. So, Dance had stepped away. Still, if she had any feeling for him, she'd call.

Yet she hadn't.

And his feelings for her hadn't faded.

"Dance?" Shannon prompted.

A muscle in his jaw bounced. He couldn't do this. "Watch the desk until Josh gets back, would you?" Without waiting on an answer, he stepped out from behind the desk and walked away.

SIXTEEN

HE wasn't sure where he was going. Somehow his feet took him straight out into the sunroom where his mom sat enjoying the sun streaming in through the glass. Dance sat on the loveseat and stared toward the flowerpot with the gardenias and pushed his hand back through his hair. "Mom. There's this girl."

His tone must have reflected his hesitation in talking about this. He felt his mom's gaze settle on him.

He rubbed his forehead. "She's got me all turned around. I don't know what to do. She's amazing, Mom. Smart, funny, and she has such a good heart. But she's totally off-limits."

"Why?"

Dance looked sidewise at his mother. She was leaning slightly forward, her face wreathed with interest and concern. She looked so much like she'd been before the stroke, his throat tightened.

"Why..?" she tried again, her frown indicating she was trying to bring out the words her brain knew, but couldn't quite get out. "Why off—?"

"She's off-limits because she has a broken heart over someone else." Dance sprang to his feet and started pacing. "She was going to marry the guy, but the jerk left her at the altar. No excuses, no warning, he simply didn't show up." Anger burned beneath his skin at that, although the alternative meant Constance would be happily married now and completely out of his reach. He actually owed the guy a huge thanks if he thought about it.

He stopped pacing, confused by his turn of thoughts, and what he was feeling.

"Do you love her?" His mom had gotten up, was standing in front of him. She'd spoken a complete unbroken sentence.

"I…" Did he love Constance? "I've only known her a little while."

"Sometimes that's all…all…all it takes."

Dance stared down at her and considered. "I feel…more for her than I've ever…" He shook his head. "But it doesn't matter. There's rules about this kind of thing."

His mom chuckled. "No rules. Not with…" She grimaced, her speech stuck inside again.

Dance really needed to hear what she had to tell him. "No rules with what, Mom?"

She lifted her face to his, eyes shiny, and slid her palm onto his chest. It felt warm through his shirt.

"The heart?" Dance nodded, more to himself than to her. "No rules when it comes to the heart."

Her hands lifted to bracket his cheeks while she stared up at him. She'd always been able to read from his expression what he had trouble saying.

"What el—else worries you?"

"Besides everything about this situation?" he drawled.

She tucked her arm in the crook of his, so they were companionably side-by-side rather than so direct. It made it easier to spill out what he was feeling. "Tell me," she prompted.

Without consciously thinking about it, they started walking slowly around the sunroom. "I do like her, Mom. More than I should. Oh, Mom, I love her."

"That scares you."

Dance frowned. He loved her. He'd said it out loud and his heart revved to life. He loved Constance Chambers. "I'm not scared." He was terrified. "Not really. It's just…I'm worried she doesn't feel the same. How can she? She loved this other guy, was set to marry him. I can't expect her to fall out of love with him and into love with me on a dime. That's not how it works. Her heart is broken. I can't be the guy who picks up all the pieces and then is left standing with them when she leaves."

His mom stopped abruptly and spun on him. Dance grabbed her elbows to steady her, but she remained firm in her stance.

"Is that what you really think?"

Dance winced at her tone. "How can I be sure?"

"Oh, honey, you can't. You simply have…have to trust. And give it time. Let your br—br—head…" Her lips firmed and she tried again. "Let your head—brain ca—catch up to…" She placed her hand over his heart again.

Dance smiled and covered her hand with his own. "Thanks, Mom. For listening."

She nodded, looking more serene and steady than he'd seen her in a long time, until her forehead wrinkled, and she moved closer to the giant planter of azaleas. "These are being overwatered."

The bell over the door chimed. From the back of the store, Constance heard Beth call out a greeting, answered by Constance's mom. And then their voices quieted to mumbling.

Brows furrowed, Constance took another shot of the antique barber's kit she had staged before she put the camera down to venture out front and see what was going on with those two.

Since their talk over cookie making, she and her mom had been closer than they had been in years, yet stopping by the shop in the middle of the afternoon wasn't a routine occurrence.

Beth and her mother were speaking quietly, heads close. They were definitely conspiring.

Constance cleared her throat and the way both jerked up like mischievous children stealing candy was comical. "What are you two up to?"

"Nothing," Beth squeaked.

Her mom recovered more swiftly. "Can't a mother take her daughter out to lunch and then a little shopping?"

"Mom, I'm working."

"Oh, piddle paddle. Beth can watch the shop. We need to get you a few new outfits suitable for travel."

"Outfits for travel. Am I going somewhere?"

Beth and her mom shared a conspiratorial look.

Constance placed her hands on her hips. "All right, give. What's going on?"

Beth dropped her gaze.

Her mom tilted her head. Never a good sign. "Beth's going to watch the shop for a few days while you go back to Texas and settle a few things with Mr. Hotel Owner."

Constance's heart fluttered like a hummingbird's. "Mom, I can't. There isn't anything to settle. If he was interested, he would have called. And it's an inn."

"Hotel, inn." Her mom waved her hand. "From what you told me, he's a gentleman. You can't expect a gentleman to make a move this fast on a woman just out of a serious relationship. Not to mention, he's southern. Southern folk are slow as molasses."

Panic tightened Constance's throat. She physically took a step back.

"It's all arranged. You leave tomorrow morning."

"But…" Her voice cracked. She tried again. "I'm scared."

"That he won't want you there?" Beth's eyes widened in disbelief. "He'd be an idiot."

"Marcus didn't want me."

"And he is an idiot." Her mom crossed her arms. Beth's mouth opened in shock, mirroring Constance's surprise. Irene Chambers had always been Team Marcus. "Besides, that doesn't count. He came back to you with his tail tucked between his knees and you booted him out."

A small grin tugged at Constance's lips, both at the image, but more that her mom was on her side. "It's not that. I'm not sure I can trust my own feelings."

"Oh, honey." In two steps her mom had Constance enfolded in a hug. "Of course you can. It just takes a little time."

Beth was there, squeezing her arm. Overwhelmed, Constance sniffled. "That's what I'm trying to give him. Some time."

Her mom pulled back, hands firmly on Constance's arms, her features set on the verge of rolling her eyes. "It takes a little time together. Not apart."

If her mom ever decided to start swatting her on the back of her head, her exasperated expression showed now would be the moment she took it up.

Who was she trying to fool? She'd never felt for Marcus anything close to what she felt for

Dance. He was her first thought in the morning, and she went to sleep wondering what he was doing.

"Go to Texas. Give it a chance," her mom said softly.

A tear wet Constance's cheek. The muscles of her belly tightened. She wanted to see him again, more than anything, but she was also afraid that he didn't return her feelings. She took in a breath and exhaled slowly. She wasn't a coward.

"Okay."

"Yes?" Beth beamed.

"Yes." Constance nodded.

"Good girl," her mom approved, her smile full of possibilities. "We'll get you several new outfits and stop by the salon—"

The bell tinkled again, and they all swiveled their heads, going silent as the object of their conversation walked into the store.

Constance gasped. Her pulse crashed against her temples and her lungs froze up so hard she couldn't take a breath.

He tipped his Stetson off, looking around the shop until his gaze met Constance's and he stopped mid-step.

Constance's heart sped up. The room seemed to close around her, narrowing in to Dance who stared with an intensity that felt like he was committing everything that was her to memory.

"Is that him?" She heard her mom ask.

"What—" Constance faltered, her legs turning to rubber. If she moved, she'd fall over. "What are you doing here?"

"I tried to give you time, let your heart heal after Marcus…" His fingers flexed and curled on the brim of his hat. "But I couldn't get you out of my head…or out of my heart. I had to come and see for myself."

"See what?" Constance's voice was small, barely audible. She clasped her hands to keep them from shaking.

Dance set his hat down brim side up on

an antique buffet and closed the distance between them. He took her trembling hands within his own. They were warm and steady. "I had to see if there was any chance that you might…" The Adam's apple in his throat column bounced. "That is, that you might somehow just a little bit, feel for me the way I feel for you."

"You came all the way for a chance?" The lump in her throat thickened.

"Yes ma'am." His sincerity shot shivers across her flesh.

"Yes."

"Ma'am?"

"Yes, there's a chance. Oh, Dance, there's more than a chance. I…I…" She looked at their joined hands, for once at a loss for words. His larger hands completely enfolded hers.

"I'm not asking for a commitment or anything, but I think we're worth a shot. I can come out here on weekends…"

"She already has a ticket." Her mom produced

an envelope and waved it between them. "Hello, Dance. I'm Constance's mother."

Dance's grin grew huge. "It's a pleasure, ma'am." He went to tip his hat before realizing he'd taken it off. His gaze slid back to Constance. "You were coming to see me?"

Constance shrugged. "Guess I was thinking about chances too."

"Dang woman." Suddenly his hands were at the small of her back and his lips were pressed over hers.

She was barely aware of her mother ushering Beth into the back room but was grateful for the privacy because as soon as they alone, Dance deepened the kiss and Constance's knees buckled.

How had she ever been unsure of her feelings for this man?

Three months later, he picked her up from the airport with a bouquet of roses. Whether she flew into Texas. or he came out to Connecticut, he always brought her flowers.

This time instead of driving to the inn, he angled the Jeep toward the winery and stopped outside. The night breeze was cool and the moon cast silver light along the grapevines.

"Is everything all right with Cletus?" she asked as Dance came around the Jeep and offered her a hand.

"'Course I'm all right. Why wouldn't I be?" Cletus answered for himself, stepping out between two of the rows of crossed timbers supporting the heavy vines. "Dance." He tipped his hat. "Constance." He opened his arms and she stepped into his hug. "Glad to see you back. When you going to make it permanent?"

It was the same question every time she came and like always, she ignored it. "How are the grapes coming along?"

"Almost ready. A few more days I think." He let her go and tipped his head again to Dance, a glimmer in his eye, and strode toward the main house before Constance could question him.

"What was that about?"

"Beats me." Dance shrugged a little too innocently and took Constance's hand, guiding her into the vineyard between the same two rows Cletus had come out of.

"Where are we going? It's dark."

"You'll be okay." Even as he said it, a glow up ahead came into view. As they got closer, Constance could tell it came from lanterns. The fragrance of ripening grapes filled the air.

"What's this?"

"You'll see." Dance pulled her along until they were close enough to see a small area lit by the light of lanterns. Nestled between the grapevine rows was a wooden bench beneath a trellised arch bursting with vines and hanging grapes. One lantern sat on top of a picnic basket on the ground while on the bench, a bucket of ice chilled a bottle of wine near two long-stemmed glasses.

Constance stopped, taking in the magical scene. It was the most romantic setting she'd ever seen. It looked like part of the vineyard, untouched by time.

"What is this place?"

Dance looked at her, his eyes warm with unguarded affection. "Clete built this decades ago for his wife. It was their together spot."

Constance placed her hand over her fluttering heart. "Their together spot." That gruff old man was the sweetest thing. "And he's letting us use it? He set this all up for us?"

Dance lifted his shoulders in a half-hearted shrug. "This place seemed fitting." The lantern's glow cast shadows across his handsome face.

"Fitting?" Her belly tingled as though she'd already sampled some of the wine.

Dance took her hand and drew her closer. "Cletus and Maddie had a wonderful marriage. He was devoted to making her happy." He looked down at their entwined fingers. A muscle jumped in his jaw. Constance's heart squeezed.

Swallowing hard, Dance looked back into her eyes. "I know we agreed to take it slow, but honey, I'm sure about us. I've never been more certain about anything." He fumbled in his pocket and pulled out a tiny velvet box.

Constance's pulse was thrumming as he lowered to one knee in the soft dirt. Her vision blurred behind a sheen of tears.

"Constance Anne Chambers, will you do me the honor of being my wife?" He opened the box. All she could see of the ring through her tears was that it sparkled in the lantern light.

Dance's voice cracked as he continued, probably unnerved that she hadn't yet answered. "I aim to devote my life making you hap—"

"Yes."

"Y-yes?" He stuttered. Actually stuttered.

"Yes." She threw her arms around him at

the same moment he was raising to scoop her up. Her chin collided with his forehead, and they stumbled apart.

Shocked, they stared at each other. Constance blinked back tears as laughter rippled through her.

Dance's husky rumble joined hers and he swung her up into his arms. "You okay?" He kissed her chin.

"I have hard bones, remember?"

He nodded, his eyes shining. "Yes? You said yes. You're going to marry me?"

She hugged him tight. "Absolutely, but you know what that means?"

He leaned back to better see her expression. He had grown wary.

She grinned, her heart still fluttery. "I get to know your name."

Relief flooded his features and his smile widened to the point a dimple appeared in his cheek. He set her feet back on the ground. "Okay, then let's do this right." He took the ring from its box and held it out to her.

It was beautiful, just right. A center diamond surrounded by smaller baguette diamonds. Simple with an understated elegance like the man who gave it to her. She extended her hand and let Dance slip it on her ring finger.

"Beverly."

Constance blinked. "What?" Was that the name of the jeweler? The cut of the diamond?

Dance grinned. "Me. I'm Beverly."

Her blinks grew more rapid.

"Beverly Atwood McCagan" He eyed her uncertainly. "The seventh."

"The seventh?" Constance hid her gasp behind her hand. "That far back?"

Dance nodded.

"Okay. Wow." She started nodding like a bobblehead. "Mrs. Beverly Atwood McCagan." Her smile warmed her down to her toes. "I can work with that."

"You can, can you?" He pulled her to him

again where she rested her cheek along his heart, marveling in the strong steady beat.

"I love you, Beverly." She sighed and felt the vibration of his chuckle.

"Coming from you, that doesn't sound so bad."

She rested her chin on his sternum to look up at him. "Because it's not. I don't see what the fuss was about."

He pressed a kiss to her upturned forehead. "You don't?"

"No, but…" She pictured a little boy with dark hair following Dance around in an over-sized cowboy hat and too-big boots. "Do we have to follow that tradition?"

Dance's grin melted her bones. "Absolutely."

Gracie's heart was heavy. Her grandmother had lived a long life, well into her nineties, yet her quick-witted grandmother left a hollow place in her heart as large as Oklahoma.

Sifting through the myriad of trunks in Grandma Maggie's attic wasn't helping her melancholy, but Camille insisted on finding the prize-winning quilt grandma had hand sewn.

Grandma was awfully proud of that quilt, so Gracie didn't think they'd find it in the attic, but they'd looked everywhere else.

"Anything over there?" Camille called from the other end of the attic. Her sister was nothing if not persistent.

"Just some old coats so far." Gracie closed the box back up and scooted it aside. There was a dusty trunk behind it, pushed under the slope of the roof. Wrinkling her nose at the dust, she pulled it out from under the eaves so she could open the lid.

A puff of white satin peaked up from beneath blue tissue paper. "Oh," Gracie cooed.

Camille's head popped up behind the larger trunks and suitcases. "Did you find it?"

"No." Gracie unfolded the tissue paper and ran her hand gingerly on the material. It was still soft to the touch. "It's a bridal gown."

Camille stopped what she was doing to come over and see for herself. "Ohh."

Camille lifted it from the trunk and held it out. The style was simple, straight lines with an empire waist. "It looks old. Was this Grandma's?"

"I don't know. It doesn't look like the gown in the photo albums." She spotted a gray envelope beneath the tissue paper and took it out from the bottom of the trunk.

"What's that?" Camille leaned over Gracie's shoulder.

Gracie pulled the flat cardstock out of the envelope and looked at the black and white photograph of her very young grandmother and a groom in uniform. "It's Grandma's wedding picture." Gracie frowned. "But that's not Grandpa with her."

"Grandma was married before Grandpa?"

Camille lowered her arms, burying her knees in folds of satin.

Gracie was as stunned as Camille. She and Grandma were close, and she'd never once said anything about another marriage before Grandpa. She turned the photograph over and read the cursive scrawled on the back.

"Peg and Eddie. May thirtieth, nineteen forty-five."

The End

Dear Reader,

I hope you enjoyed book 1 in the *Chapel Pines* series. I love this little imaginary town and wish I could live there. Next up is Wyatt's story where he meets an introvert looking for answers to her grandmother's hidden past. Theirs is a slow burn where even that is a little fast for Gracie.

When I wrote this series, I got so many letters from fans thanking me for these books. As an author, I love feedback. You are the reason that I've brought these characters together and am continuing to write. So, tell me what you liked, what you loved, even what drove you crazy. I'd love to hear from you. You can visit me on the web at www.cloverautrey.com

Appreciated greatly,

Clover Autrey

ABOUT THE AUTHOR

Clover Autrey has a very clear memory of being on a swing set, thinking that being a writer must be the most wonderful job in the world. She was right.

She enjoys writing quick easy reads with lots of bromance and male banter as the guys find their ladies and their happily ever afters.

If you enjoyed this book, please leave a review. Reviews are like little golden pats on the back sprinkled in fairy dust. Trust me, we authors appreciate them more than you realize.

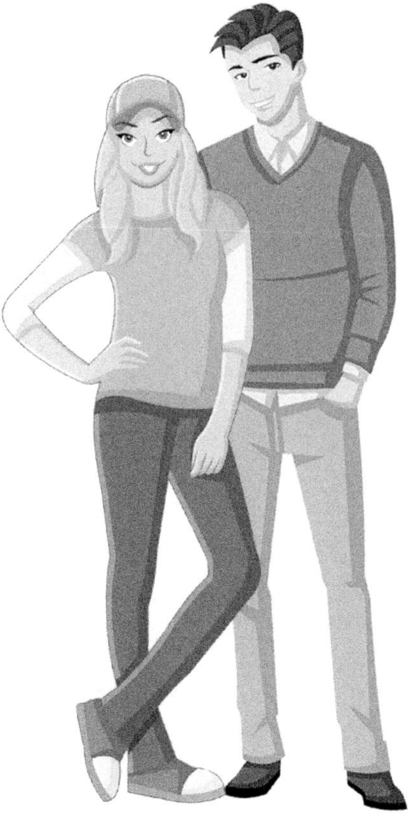

Printed in Great Britain
by Amazon